MERARI

BY THE AUTHOR

Rahab: A Novel

KD

MERARI

The Woman Who Challenged Queen Jezebel and the Pagan Gods

Gloria Howe Bremkamp

1817

Harper & Row, Publishers, San Francisco
Cambridge, Hagerstown, New York, Philadelphia
London, Mexico City, São Paulo, Singapore, Sydney

FIRST EDITION

Designed by Donald Hatch

Library of Congress Cataloging-in-Publication Data

Bremkamp, Gloria Howe.
    Merari: the woman who challenged Queen Jezebel and the Pagan gods.

    I. Title.
PS3552.R369M47   1986   813'.54   85–45349
ISBN 0–06–061049–2

86 87 88 89 90 HC 10 9 8 7 6 5 4 3 2 1

For my friend
GERALDINE SANDERS CLARK,
who admired the Shunammite woman,
and whose own faith was
deep, abiding, and
inspirational
to all who knew her.

"One day Elisha went to Shunem. And a well-to-do woman was there, who urged him to stay for a meal. So whenever he came by, he stopped there to eat. She said to her husband, "I know that this man who often comes our way is a holy man of God. Let's make a small room on the roof and put in it a bed and a table, a chair and a lamp for him. Then he can stay there whenever he comes to us."

2 Kings 4:8–10
New International Version

-1-

Merari's first glimpse of Joram in the royal procession startled her. The years seemed scarcely to have changed him. He was heavier. More muscular. His clean-shaven face was weathered and tanned. And he still looked more like the reckless youth of her memories than like the leader of a powerful nation.

"The king is come! Long live the King!"

The chant spilled forth, cascaded through the crowded outer courtyard of the Ivory Palace, and drifted on across the city of Samaria to the ancient hills beyond.

For the second time in a year, the Northern Kingdom of Israel was seeing the coronation of a son of the late King Ahab, and his queen, Jezebel. Merari grimaced, uncomfortable at being here and dreading the likelihood that she would have to speak to Joram. Years before, she had sworn never again to get near him. She'd kept her vow. Until today. Strong family pressures finally had induced her to come, in spite of her better judgment.

"Don't be a goose, Merari!" her mother had scolded. "You have to come with us. Your father is still Royal Minister of Trade. Your husband is still Royal Overseer of the Lands of Shunem and Megiddo."

"And Uncle Obadiah is still Master of the Royal Palaces," Nahum interjected in his customary tone of dutiful earnestness. "It will be most embarrassing, my wife, if you are not with us at the coronation."

She relented, of course—even though her usual certainty that all would be well had deserted her. What else could she do? Her mother's urgings had been expected. But Nahum's agreement surprised her. It was ironic that she should be here, feeling as she did.

The procession came closer, moved through the shadowy coolness of a far arcade, and reemerged into the glistening sunlight of the outer courtyard. Steadily it came forward, past the great fountain, past the abominable altar and the pillar of Baal. That particular feature of the huge courtyard had been there since her longest memory. A testament of cruelty. A symbol of suspicion and mistrust. A constant reminder of the ever-pervasive conflict between Baal worship and belief in the Lord God Jehovah. It was, indeed, ironic to be here again.

Trumpets blared, then softened to allow the sounds of lyre and timbrels to rise in a musical salute. The crowd began again to chant.

Merari remained silent. Even Joram's being here as a king in coronation was ironic. He had never wanted to be king. "As second son, I am safe from such a fate," he used to boast. "Let brother Ahaziah play king. He wants that kind of glory. And he will do whatever our beloved mother tells him to do. I will be a warrior, a charioteer. Nothing more."

The fact that his older brother's glory as king was short-lived dashed his fondest dreams of a warrior's life. Following the death of their father, Ahab, in battle at Ramoth-Gilead, Ahaziah became king. But he had been on the throne of the Northern Kingdom of Israel for less than a year when a strange and foolish accident had taken his life. Some members of the royal court, including Merari's father and Nahum's Uncle Obadiah, suspected treachery. Loyalists to the Queen Mother Jezebel held strong wishes for her to rule the kingdom instead of her oldest son. But other people, especially the holy man, Elisha, considered the death an act of righteous retribution against the house of Ahab and Jezebel and all their offspring as ordained by the Lord God Jehovah.

It was no wonder Joram wanted only to be a warrior and

a charioteer. He probably thought that would be one way to avoid the wrath of the Lord. "Not that I believe in your Lord," he had once told her. "How could anything unseen be as powerful as you and your friend, Elisha, claim this God to be?" They had argued then, as they always seemed to, about the existence of the Lord and about whether a person could hide from him. She had accused Joram of being irresponsible, and of being rough and uncaring. He had laughed and turned away.

But now he was a king, not a reckless boy. Now whatever he believed about the Lord would affect an entire nation. And now how he behaved personally, could affect her and her family. Was he still irresponsible? An involuntary shiver went through her. Why should she wonder such a thing now? Why should it matter? She long since had determined to have nothing more to do with him. Why, indeed, should she wonder whether he was still rough and uncaring?

"Merari? Are you all right?" Nahum asked, moving up next to her so she could hear him over the din of the crowd.

She straightened as he repeated the question; then nodded uncertainly.

"Memories?"

"Yes." She glanced up at him, grateful that he understood.

Joram was approaching quite near to them now.

Nahum moved protectively closer to her.

She remained motionless, pinned by the direct penetration of Joram's gaze. A sardonic smile played at his mouth. Did she imagine it, or did he hesitate for half a second?

A muttered curse escaped from Nahum.

Close by her other side, her mother made graceful obeisance to the new king, and whispered, "Salaam, Merari. Salaam."

But she continued to stand motionless, watching the procession carry Joram away from her toward the entrance to the magnificent throne room and on into the recesses of the palace.

"Oh, your poor father's job. Really, Merari, the least you could do is put on an act of courtesy for the new king." Zibia's face was flushed. Her birdlike hands made a futile, helpless gesture.

Merari grasped her mother's hands and gently cradled them in her own. "I'll not play the hypocrite over Joram. You know that."

"But . . . your father."

"Father doesn't expect it."

"What about Nahum? You know how Joram hates him."

"I'm not that important to Joram," Nahum countered.

Zibia started again to protest, but Nahum interceded on Merari's behalf: "And Uncle Obadiah is too important for Joram to harm him. Who else in the palace will stand with him against Jezebel? Especially now that he is king?"

Zibia appeared to give up.

Merari let go of her hands. "You see, Mother, we feel differently than you. Some things we will not compromise on."

"But . . . my dear child."

Merari shook her head. "No. I will not play the hypocrite over Joram. I fear you have been the wife of a diplomat too long."

Zibia bridled, then apparently thought better of it. The coronation procession had disappeared inside the entryway to the throne room. Zibia pulled her shawl more firmly about her shoulders and turned to follow. As she moved away, she said over her shoulder, "I certainly hope you don't make a scene inside, Merari. After all, you are still a diplomat's daughter!"

Her mother's reaction was typical, thought Merari. Take the last word and walk away. Deny the chance for reply. Discussion closed. She wished that she could treat life's situations that way. And she wished, too, that she could be that casual about her priorities between family and politics and between personal likes and dislikes. It would make life much simpler. In this immediate situation, it would ease her dread of having to see Joram again, and maybe even having to speak to him.

"Come along, beloved," urged Nahum, walking toward the palace.

Reluctantly, she followed.

They caught up with Zibia just inside the entryway, where servants were helping guests remove their footwear and fitting them with soft slippers that wouldn't mar the inlaid ivory floors. At almost the same moment, one of her father's aides came up to them and bowed deeply. Turning to Zibia he said, "Madam, your husband, the Honorable Benaiah, has instructed me to escort you, your daughter, and your son-in-law to the royal dais, where he is in attendance to the king." He made a rather grandiose gesture toward the opposite end of the enormous hall. "Honorable Benaiah has further instructed me to ask you to proceed with all haste. King Joram wishes to greet you all personally."

Merari felt her heart sink. The dread came full surface. She should never have come; in spite of all the family pressures, she should have avoided this confrontation. Momentary panic tempted her with flight. She glanced about. There was no place to run. Hiding in the crowd would only create the scene her mother had warned against. This she would not allow to happen.

After all, she was her father's own daughter. On more than one occasion, her sense of diplomacy and standing fast in tense situations had prevailed. It must prevail now. All is well, she told herself. All is well. She took a deep breath and stood tall. Her mother and Nahum were looking at her, direct and questioning. She responded with a steady look and silence.

Across Zibia's face, a tiny smile, hinting of smugness, appeared briefly and vanished. She turned to the aide. "Come. We mustn't keep the king waiting, must we?"

They proceeded toward the royal dais over floors of inlaid ivory and decorative mosaics of semiprecious stones as richly patterned as parquetry. To the right, through an ornately carved archway, the banqueting hall was visible. Long tables, laden with an extravagant array of foods, were being fussed over by scurrying servants under the watchful eyes of the Banquet Masters. The thought of food choked Merari. Quickly, she looked away.

To the left was the long, narrow gallery that paralleled the king's private inner courtyard and led beyond to the royal chambers. Inlaid ivory and mosaic floors extended into both the gallery and the courtyard. Fountains sparkled amid cool, green beauty of flowering shrubbery. Birds flitted in and out of the shrubbery's shelter.

A swift shaft of childhood memory darted through Merari's mind. What safe, good memories she once had of this place. Her father and mother had often brought her here when she was a child to play with Joram and his sister, Athaliah. Their friendship had been a close one. As toddlers, they had romped and tussled together. Later, they had laughed and teased over blindman's bluff, learned to read and write together, hidden from the scribe who was their teacher, and mourned together over the death of a tiny bird they had made their pet. Those memories of her childhood friendship with Joram and Athaliah were such good ones.

It was the later memories—memories of young adulthood—that were clouded with anger and fear. The innocence and openness of their friendship had slowly disintegrated as they became young adults. They had grown apart. Athaliah, who was two years older, had discovered boys quite early, liked them in an openly lustful way, and had soon became the object of a politically expedient marriage to the Prince Regent Jehoram of the Southern Kingdom of Judah.

Joram had changed, too, from a mischievous, fun-loving boy to a reckless, self-centered youth. He had involved himself in the orgies of Baal worship as a way to prove his manhood until he discovered charioteering, which seemed to more than satisfy his lust for reckless adventure and to reinforce his perception of himself as a masterful man.

Thinking back over the years, Merari reminded herself that she had changed, too.

More and more, her parents found reasons why she should travel with them on diplomatic-trade missions, or visit her aunt in Joppa on the coast of Philistia, or spend months at a time in the house at Shunem. Only later did she realize that the trips and the long sojourns in Shunem were deliberately planned to separate her from the association and the influence of Athaliah and Joram.

One day when they had returned from a trip and were settling into the house in Shunem, she asked her father about it.

"Their friendship is no longer good for you, Merari," he answered in an uncharacteristically stern tone.

She looked puzzled.

"We're in a peculiar position," he explained. "During all the years of my service to the royal court, your mother and I have never agreed with Ahab and Jezebel's religious beliefs. Nor, for that matter, with their way of living their private lives, or raising their children."

Astonishment coursed through her. He sounded absolutely disloyal. She'd never thought that her father could be disloyal. But was he? Was he a hypocrite?

Seeing her reaction, Benaiah rushed on. "We have simply shut our eyes to a lot of things, Merari. But now that you're growing into womanhood, we don't want you involved in court life. You would be miserable."

"But what about you, Father? And Mother?"

"As I said, we have simply shut our eyes to a lot of things. We always have."

"But why?"

"Because we like the ease and comfort that my position as a royal minister brings to us."

She said nothing.

"Do you understand?"

She nodded. But she didn't really understand. And after her father had gone into another part of the house, she unsuccessfully fought back hot tears of disillusionment.

Nahum, in search of Benaiah, found her instead and comforted her. "All of life is a compromise, one way or another," he said. "The secret is to learn to cope with it. That's all your father has done. If it came down to a principle, though, he would stand firm, just as my Uncle Obadiah would. That's why they've been such good friends for so long. They're both men of principle."

"Are you a man of principle, too?"

"Would it make a difference if I weren't?"

She searched his face, and realized that it would. The only nephew of Obadiah, the powerful Master of the Royal Palaces, he had been a family friend for many years. When her father had decided to move the family from the royal court at Samaria to the house at Shunem, he had asked that Nahum be appointed Royal Overseer of the Lands of Shunem and Megiddo. The request had been granted, and Nahum had become an everyday part of their lives.

He was eight years her senior, and she regarded him as a strong, dependable older brother. But as they spent more and more time together, her feelings toward him began to change.

"When we're so different," she asked one day as they walked beside a small tributary of the River Zalud, "why do you you think we're so attracted to each other?"

He tossed a small pebble into the stream and grinned. "*Are* we attracted to each other?"

She stopped, glanced up at him ready to argue, and then realized he was teasing her. She made a face.

He laughed, and with strong brown fingers lifted her chin so she was forced to look directly at him. "It's probably only a case of friendship, or of hero worship. I'm too old for you."

- 8 -

She frowned. If what she was beginning to feel for him was friendship, it was different from any other she had ever known. And she didn't worship him as a hero. But she couldn't tell him either of those things. Just being around him seemed to arouse strange new emotions that she didn't fully understand.

He continued to gaze at her for another brief moment thinking how innocently attractive she was. Her shoulder-length hair, ash-blonde in color, was neatly combed and tied with a blue ribbon. Her skin was smooth and tanned; her eyes wide-set and a clear aquamarine in color. Her mouth, full and generous, smiled most of the time; but not now.

He took his fingers away from her chin and laughed again. "Don't look so solemn. When people are friends, they find each other attractive."

"Then you do find me attractive?" she quickly countered.

He straightened and backed off, feigning shock. "I confess to nothing except a feeling of friendship."

"But, you said—"

"I know what I said," he defended in good humor. "You're trying to trick me, I think."

She pretended to pout. "Why would I do that?"

He leaned down, picked up another pebble and sailed it through the still air of late afternoon.

She heard the pebble hit the water at a distance. "Why would I do that?" she repeated, feeling again the new sensation inside herself—and yet not moving one inch toward him.

He turned and looked at her with an expression she'd never before seen in his eyes. It was an expression that seemed to probe the depths of her very being, as if, by some miracle of the supernatural, he would be able to discern her most secret thoughts.

A shout interrupted the mood.

Startled, they turned. It was Kallai, Nahum's oldest friend and chief assistant. "Nahum, Merari, come at once! We have a guest."

They walked toward him, curious about what visitor could bring such a stern summons.

"It's Joram," Kallai blurted. He's come to see you, Merari!"

A shiver of trepidation went through her.

Nahum's face grew strangely dark and brooding. "What does he want with Merari?"

"It's probably only a casual visit," Merari reassured him. "All will be well. You'll see."

But all was not well. When she entered the main salon of the house, the air was fraught with tension. She was glad Nahum had gone off with Kallai instead of coming into the house with her. Joram sat in her mother's prized Egyptian chair, which Benaiah had bought for her in Thebes. Her mother, hands folded in her lap, sat motionless just beyond. To the left, her father stood staring gloomily at a huge, untouched platter of fruits and cheeses on a low round table. He glanced up at Merari. "Come in, my daughter."

Joram squirmed about in the chair and gave her a questioning look. Apparently, he had brought unwelcome news. She hoped it had nothing to do with her. She came forward carefully.

"Border fighting has broken out again. Joram stopped to tell us. He's on his way to Megiddo to alert the chariot corps," explained Benaiah.

"But I also wanted to see you, Merari." He surveyed her in a calculating, discomfiting way from head to foot and back again. "Everyone at the royal court misses you," he said. "When are you coming back?"

She looked to her father for an answer.

Benaiah stepped forward, and in his best diplomat's tone promised, "After next harvest, perhaps. But, come now, we have not done you full honor, young man. Before you go on to Megiddo, we must give you a meal."

Joram declined. "I have no time for food, sir. But I would like to show off my new chariot and team to Merari. I would make time for that." He looked at her questioningly again. She hesitated.

"That's a splendid idea," her father pressed. "You'd like that, wouldn't you Merari?"

"Of course, father," she said, wondering if her reluctance was obvious.

Apparently, to Joram, it was not. He said hurried goodbyes to Benaiah and Zibia and led Merari down the gallery toward the entryway, already bragging about his horses and his war chariot.

He was skillful at handling the animals, and he liked driving fast. Like the wind, they rode over the rolling hills and down across the Plain of Jezreel. Merari felt excitement rise inside her. This was fun. Joram was fun. In a way, she almost wished that she and her parents still lived in the Ivory Palace in Samaria. She could be with him more then. Forgetting time, they drove and laughed until dusk had almost fully settled over the land. They stopped then in an olive grove to cool the horses, and to refresh themselves with a drink from a nearby cistern. Laughing and teasing, their spirits high with the excitement of the moment, they began a water fight. In another instant, they were tussling with each other as they had so often done when they were children. She thought nothing of it.

She had not meant to lead him on. And had not realized she was doing so, until suddenly he grabbed her, pulling her down beside him in the deepest shadows of an ancient olive tree. The childlike quality of their play had vanished.

She resisted.

He persisted. His mouth found hers.

She struggled.

He wrestled with her, passion rising.

She panicked and cried out.

He forced her down, flat on the ground, pressed his lean,

strong body against her in savage demand, and with one hand began to fumble with her clothing.

Fear shot through her. She struggled harder.

It was then that Nahum arrived. He pulled Joram off her, shoved him aside with a threatening curse, and ordered him to leave.

Joram stumbled up onto his feet and shook off Nahum's hard, tight grip. A half-wild look glazed his eyes. Breathless and muttering, he cursed the older man: "I'll have her, damn you. You're nothing but a farmer. I'm a prince!"

Nahum shoved him toward the chariot. "Get off this land!"

"She's mine!"

Nahum stepped toward him threateningly.

"Even if I have to marry her, I'll have her!"

"I'll kill you first!"

Joram ran from him, clambered aboard the chariot, and whipped the startled horses into a run in the direction of Megiddo.

Merari, breathless from fright and still on the ground where Joram had thrown her, stared after him, and then up at Nahum.

Indignation flamed in his face. He gasped for breath, taking in great gulps of air, chest heaving and feet firmly planted on the royal lands of Shunem, in the great Plain of Jezreel.

Disbelief coursed through Merari. If she had ever consciously thought about needing proof of how she felt about either Joram or Nahum, she had it now.

"He might do it, you know." Her voice trembled.

"What?"

"Force me to marry him."

"Your father will never let it happen."

"If King Ahab decrees it . . ." She hid her face in her hands and began to cry.

Nahum came to her, knelt down, and took her in his arms. For several moments, they clung to each other, knowing that the danger to Nahum was as great as to her. Maybe greater. He had threatened to kill a prince of the royal house.

Through misty eyes, she searched his face. "I'm afraid for you."

"And I for you." He kissed her gently on the forehead.

"We need to get to my father and tell him everything. He will help us."

"Will he let me marry you?"

The question caught her by surprise. She pushed away from him and searched his face. Was he teasing? And if not, how should she answer? He was older, and that seemed to bother him more than it did her. He was a farmer, a man of the land. Could she be satisfied to live the rest of her life here in the Plain of Jezreel? Did she love him enough to do that? And to have his children? And to care for him when he was even older, and perhaps sick?

So long did she stare at him, all these questions going through her mind, that he misread her reaction. He let go of her with a sigh and sat down on the ground beside her. "You don't want to marry me, do you?"

"I didn't say that," she countered.

Hope flared again in his eyes.

"In truth, I think I've loved you for a very long time."

Her parents and Nahum's Uncle Obadiah not only approved of their decision to marry, but hurriedly set about making all the necessary arrangements in order to be sure that Joram would make no trouble for them with his father, King Ahab. Much later, they learned that after the incident in the olive grove, Joram had gone on a drinking spree in Megiddo. Shortly afterward, King Ahab had ordered his chariot corps, including Joram, detached to Jericho, and following that, he had appointed Joram as his personal liaison to the court of the King of Sidon.

In all the intervening years since their marriage, Merari and Nahum had not seen Joram. Benaiah, who saw him on occasion during trips to Sidon, came back with reports that

Joram had grown into a mature man with no malice toward either of them. Merari often wondered at the full truth of that. She didn't remember Joram as a forgiving person.

Now, seeing him again on this day of his coronation, with the surge of old memories so sharply focused in her mind, she wished more fervently than ever that she had stayed in Shunem.

They were quite near the royal dais by this time. Her father's aide was excusing himself, and her father was coming to greet them. He would present them formally to the royal family in the prescribed custom. The crowd of other guests had thinned. In fact, it appeared that they were among the last to pay their respects to the royal personages. Nahum stepped aside to speak with his Uncle Obadiah. With her mother, she made a deep bow to the Queen Mother Jezebel and then greeted Athaliah and her oldest son, Ahaziah of Judah. Her mother and father paused to chat; and she found herself alone with Joram and unable now to avoid a face-to-face meeting.

Joram seemed to welcome the opportunity. He stepped off the dais and came to her. "You're still very beautiful, Merari."

His voice had lost all traces of boyishness, and by inflection seemed to reveal unexpected kindness. But could she trust it? The familiar calculating look was in his eyes. Seeing it, she was reminded how quickly his mood could change. Embarrassed, she bowed to him.

He extended his hand to help her rise.

Mistrusting, she ignored it and took a step backward.

"You can't *still* be angry with me. Not after all these years!"

Her heart pounded.

"Do you have not even a single word of greeting for an old friend?"

Hot and flustered, she didn't know what to say.

As her silence lengthened, Joram's face darkened with

irritation. "It seems that your marriage to an old man who can give you no children has broken your spirit!"

Anger welled up inside her.

He gave a scornful laugh and circled her with an inspective eye, as if judging a prize animal. "Now that I'm king, I may once again pursue you. Just to teach you to talk to me."

"Won't you ever grow up, Joram?" Athaliah intervened. "Stop badgering Merari. She's a married woman now." An appreciative light filtered into her eyes as she watched Nahum coming toward them. "And, I might add, she's married to a very attractive man."

Joram ignored his sister, and once more circled Merari. "Yes, now that I'm king, I have more options to get what I want. You might tell that to the old farmer you married." He spun about on his heel and made off toward the banquet hall.

Inwardly, Merari sagged, relieved that Joram had left but humiliated by his attitude, regretting her own reactions, and fearful of the threat implied in his parting words.

-2-

Nahum's gentle kiss awakened Merari. Darkness still cloaked the house in Shunem. Only the night lamp flickering in its clay saucer on a side chest interrupted the darkness and cast Nahum's shadow larger than life against the far wall of their sleeping alcove. Once more, he brushed her forehead with a light kiss; then he got up to begin dressing for the day's work in the barley fields. Harvest was in full swing.

She stretched. Then lay back for another delicious, drifting moment of half-wakefulness. It was good to be back in their own home, in their own room, even though the days here began before dawn. It was so unlike the routine of the palace in Samaria, where late rising was not only acceptable but expected. In the evenings, late dining and even later entertainment were the custom in the palace. It seemed that it was a place where people constantly struggled to force their own timing and their own will on the things of nature. Her father had been right all those years before to move them out of that environment. Here in Shunem, life was much more simple and uncomplicated. Here the land and its natural cycles set human schedules. It was good to be back. Away from the pretensions of the capital city. Away from from the artificial courtesy and gaiety of the Ivory Palace. And away from Joram!

Even though she'd had only the single confrontation with him, she knew there was more to come. Joram would not give up easily. Her silence had offended him. She thought repeatedly about his words, "Now that I'm king, I have more options to get what I want." It was true; he *did* have options. Nor did she doubt his intention to use them. When that would occur, of course, remained to be seen. The most obvious option would be for him to refuse to reappoint Nahum as Royal Overseer of the Lands of Shunem and Megiddo. That would be direct and vengeful. Less direct, but equally vengeful, would be to revoke the appointments of her father and Uncle Obadiah. She doubted he would do that, however: he needed both of them. He needed Nahum, too, but he would never admit it.

Her father and Uncle Obadiah had both tried to convince her that her fears were groundless. "With all the unrest on our borders, Joram needs your father's negotiating skills more than ever," assured Uncle Obadiah.

"Nor will he throw out Obadiah as long as Jezebel is alive. Obadiah is his buffer," her father pointed out. "And as far as Nahum's reappointment is concerned, Joram will allow practical politics to prevail. The production of food-stuffs from this valley is vital, and Nahum has made it more productive than ever before."

In the days following, Merari thought often about what they had said. Although she tried hard to dredge up some semblance of conviction that they were right, the old unset-tled feeling stayed with her. She simply was not able to rid herself of the notion that in some way, at some time, Joram would take vindictive action. Now that recurring thought brought her fully awake. She pushed back the coverlet and sat up. The predawn air was cool. She shivered.

Nahum turned, grinned at her, and tossed her a home-spun robe.

She shrugged into it, swung around and dangled her legs over the side of the bed, then stretched them straight out in front of her and made a circling motion with her feet.

"All is well?" Nahum pulled the leather girdle about his waist and buckled it.

"All is well!" She stood up, went to him, and kissed him full on the mouth.

He put his arms around her and pulled her close. She

pressed against him, soaking up the warmth of his body and the strength of his spirit. "I thank God for you, my husband."

"And I for you, beloved."

For yet another long moment, they stood enclosed in each other's embrace, savoring the safety and comfort and acceptance mutually provided.

"Walk to the gate with me?" Nahum whispered, pulling away.

She took his hand and followed him through the silent house, across the courtyard to the outer gate where Kallai waited with some of the foremen and with the horses. At Nahum's appearance, the men all mounted and, with a salute to Merari, headed out for the tasks of the day.

The sun still hid its face behind the heights of Mount Moreh. But beyond the wide shadow cast by the mountain, pale light spilled unevenly across the great valley floor, defining the barley and wheat fields stretching away toward the distant horizon like some great golden sea.

Her father called it "Israel's coveted cupboard at the crossroads," and certainly it was all of that. The bounty of its yield in fruits and grains, olives and vegetables, was unparalleled in all of Israel. It was of equal importance as a corridor for international trade and covetous armies. Of all the wide, fertile valleys distinguishing the mountainous Northern Kingdom of Israel, this one, the Jezreel Valley, was most conspicuous, most easily accessible, most productive. By virtue of its shape, size, and location, it was thoroughly entitled to be called "the great valley."

Its shape roughly resembled a giant wineskin laid on its side. A gentle curve from the southeast at the Jordan rift, just north of Beth-shan, to the northwest opened out into the Plain of Accho in Phoenicia. The Carmel range of mountains flanked it on the west and southwest. Mount Gilboa and Mount Moreh defined its eastern limits at two important points. The city of Jezreel, location of Jezebel's summer palace, was situated across the western slopes of

Gilboa a dozen miles due south of Shunem. Shunem itself nestled on the lower slopes of Mount Moreh and commanded a magnificent view of the widest portion of the valley. To the southwest, across the valley seven or eight miles, was Megiddo, the great fortress which dominated the saddlelike pass through the Carmel Mountains. The pass provided a direct route for merchant caravans and invading armies alike from the north to the coastal cities of Philistia, and on to Egypt, Nubia, and beyond.

Merari studied the plain from west to east and back again, thinking how peaceful it looked. It was hard to imagine the need for a fortress like Megiddo. It was equally difficult to comprehend the number of armies which had fought over the valley for thousands of years, or to visualize the number of lives given up in the name of holy war in order to dominate the land guarded by Megiddo.

And yet the very ground on which she was standing had felt the impact of many battles between many great armies. Even those of King Saul, when he had come against her mother's own people, the Philistines. In fact, the land still owned by her mother and father originally had come to her mother's family as booty from the battle in which King Saul and his son lost their lives. The land, so beautiful and so bountiful, was too valuable not to be fought over. With a sigh, she acknowledged the need for a fortress like Megiddo. And for warriors. And for chariots of war. And for charioteers like Joram.

His reign would not be a peaceful one, she reflected. He was not a man of peace. Nor was he a man of God. Maybe that's what had bothered her most about him always. He gave true allegiance to no one except himself.

With a sigh of uncertainty, she turned to go back into the house. The full light of morning had crept in on slippered feet. Nahum and the others long since had disappeared into the furthest fields. The road in front of the house, which led off westwardly to the Carmel Mountains, was deserted. The enormous shadow cast earlier by Mount Moreh had diminished. A golden haze, sheer and soft, now filtered across the courtyard and into part of the house.

Enough of this standing about, she told herself. There was much to be done. Grain baskets had to be sorted and counted. Winnowing forks needed to be made ready for the threshers. Jars for the olive crop had to be checked. The trees were more heavily laden with fruit this year than usual. New jars would be needed, no doubt, for both the olives and their oil. And since the olive harvest would begin within the passing of another two moons, she must talk to the potters and get them started making new jars. And then there were the baskets for the grapes, and new wineskins to be checked. Harvest! The busiest season of all. There was much to be done.

She went back into the house, washed and dressed, and then made her way through the main part of the house. A peaceful hush, suitable companion to the softness of the early morning light, pervaded it. Most of the servants had gone with Nahum and Kallai to help with the harvest. Her parents' wing of the house was all quiet, too. Her father had been summoned to a meeting at the Ivory Palace in Samaria. Her mother was indulging herself by sleeping late. From the back of the house, though, she heard the cooks moving about, and suddenly she smelled baking bread. Hunger gnawed at her. She headed down the long gallery leading to the cooking area.

"My mistress, wait!"

She glanced about. Tamar hurried after her. "I thought you had gone to the fields with the others."

The woman nodded. "I started with them, . . . but . . ."

Merari laughed. "Wait, catch your breath." Tamar had served her since they both were in their teens. Now, she was more friend than servant. And like all the others who served this household, she was a free person. Customary as it was to have slaves, Benaiah did not believe in slavery. Neither did Nahum. As a result, they hired only free men and women to work the place. Tamar's whole family had worked for them at one time or another. Her father had been in charge of the tannery and the making of the wineskins from goat hides. Her mother had cooked for the household. Her sisters and two brothers had worked in the pottery shed and as herdsmen. Now they were all gone except Tamar. Her parents were dead; her sisters had married and moved away; the two brothers had fought and died at Ramoth-Gilead alongside King Ahab. This left Tamar more than ever a part of the family. "Now that you have caught your breath," Merari laughed again, "tell me where you have come from with obviously exciting news."

"From the village."

"Your news must be very important."

"It is. It is!" Tamar's dark eyes glistened with excitement. "This will be a specially blessed day."

"Then tell me."

"The seer."

"What seer?"

"The Holy One. The new prophet."

"You mean Elisha?"

"Yes, the prophet Elisha."

"What about him?"

"He comes."

"Here?"

Tamar nodded.

"When?"

"Today!"

Momentary concern overrode Merari's surprise. Elisha had been their friend for many years. He came from the village where her father had been born, Abel-meholah, beyond the Jordan. He was not much older than she was. Yet he carried the wisdom and the responsibilities of a man many years her senior. This would be his first visit to the house in Shunem since he had received the mantle of spiritual leadership from the prophet Elijah. While he was more than welcome, and while it would be wonderful to have him visit, he was now an important personage. The household was not prepared for such an important visitor.

"You're sure he's coming today?"

Tamar nodded.

"Then we must prepare for him. My mother must be awakened and asked to help us. Someone must go to the fields and tell Nahum so that he will come home as soon as possible. A room must be prepared for our guest . . . and food. What about food, Tamar? Is there plenty prepared? Or must we . . ." A sudden and irrelevant question popped into her mind. She probed Tamar's face. "How did you know about this news so early in the day?"

Tamar blushed, revealing the answer without a single word. Only one person could provoke such a reaction in Tamar: Elisha's servant, Gehazi. She was in love with him. Gehazi, on the other hand, while quick to accept all the gifts that such a feeling generated, often seemed reluctant to respond in kind. Perhaps it was because Tamar was so guileless in her generosity that Gehazi felt it his natural right to accept everything and give nothing in return. Or perhaps, it was that Gehazi prompted Tamar into giving more and more, that he simply and deliberately used her. Whichever it was, the relationship worried Merari. She feared that Tamar would be hurt. "Where is Gehazi?"

"With the prophet at the house of the elder priest in Shunem."

"Well, then, how did he . . . ?"

Tamar blushed. "He saw me walking with the others to the fields this morning. And he called to me, and . . ." She paused, as if reflecting on the incident with abnormal interest.

"And then what?"

"Then he sent me here to alert the household about his master's intentions of visiting us."

"He sent you?"

Tamar nodded.

"Was he too busy to come himself?"

She looked puzzled. "Should he not have sent me?"

"Never mind. It isn't important." Merari walked on with Tamar following.

"Gehazi is very loyal, my mistress.

"He is also bossy." Merari said.

They had reached the cooking area by this time. The aroma of freshly baked bread was overpowering. "I'm starved," Merari announced to everyone within earshot. The servants reacted with their usual respect and hurried to place food on the long wooden table at one side of the area. Tamar brought a pitcher of cool, fresh goat's milk from the spring cellar and set it on the table in front of her.

Merari thanked them, broke off a small chunk of the still-warm bread, and began to eat.

Tamar meanwhile announced rather officiously that the prophet Elisha was coming to be a guest in the house, and began instructing the kitchen servants about the foods that would be needed. Merari couldn't help but notice what a surprisingly good imitation Tamar was giving of Gehazi. But she made no effort to stop her. The kitchen servants would take care of that in their own good time.

She finished her meal and sent Tamar out to the fields to tell the news of Elisha's arrival to Nahum while she herself went in to awaken her mother.

"Will you take charge of the household preparations? Elisha could arrive at any time. In the next few minutes, or at the close of day. You know how he is. Stopping and talking with everyone he sees."

"Well, if he's staying at the house of the elder priest, he'll not arrive here until nightfall," Zibia said. "That old man can talk the stripes off a zebra."

As it turned out, Zibia was right. Elisha didn't arrive until late afternoon shadows had crept across the valley floor and the day's oppressive heat had started to diminish. An errant breeze now and again touched the faces of the flowering shrubs in the courtyard where the family had gathered to greet him.

Servants came with trays of fruits and cheeses, drinking cups, and a large carafe of wine. Gehazi and Tamar, along with the small retinue which had followed Elisha into the compound, had disappeared toward the back of the house.

Merari sat down opposite Elisha, reminding herself how much he was like Nahum, in spite of the differences in their appearances. Elisha was unpretentious, straightforward, hard-working and dependable as the days of summer were long. All these qualities he shared with Nahum. But there the likeness ended.

In physical appearance, they were quite different. Nahum was tall and lean with a full head of dark, wavy hair just beginning to gray at the temples. He wore no beard. His eyes were the color of a placid summer sky.

Elisha, on the other hand, was shorter, stockier. His eyes were the color of charcoal embers. From time to time, the expression in the eyes brightened, the embers sparking into flame, giving him the fiery look of the fanatic. He wore a neatly trimmed beard. But his hairline receded so far that he could be considered bald. In fact, the natural recession resembled the strictly tonsured look traditionally forbidden to good Hebrews. What a folly of nature! A bald Hebrew prophet who fought pagan priests who, in turn, deliberately shaved their heads as a symbol of the idolatrous practices of Baal worship! What folly indeed.

"We're pleased to have you as our guest again, Elisha." Merari smiled at him. "We're going to be very selfish and have just a quiet family gathering with you tonight."

Nahum offered him a cup of wine. "There's much we want to visit about with you."

"Good. We've had no chance to talk at all since Joram became king."

"Were you at the coronation?"

He nodded.

"Strange we didn't see you."

"Jezebel kept a close watch over us." Elisha grinned.

"Not one waking moment was I left alone. Nor, for that matter, was my man, Gehazi."

"Jezebel is scared to death of you," Zibia interjected. "That's the reason for the constant surveillance."

"Would that such fear could turn her from her evil ways," Elisha answered.

"Now that Joram is king, some people are wondering if she will be as powerful as before," Nahum said. "Is that just a local feeling? Or have you heard that elsewhere?"

Elisha thought for a moment. "Idolatrous practices still go on everywhere in the kingdom. And the royal court seems to sanction them."

"We hear much about the miracles you are performing," Merari said. "That should have some effect."

Elisha nodded. "It's true. The Lord God is using me in many ways as an instrument of his power."

"Then you *did* smite the waters of The Jordan with Elijah's mantle and make them part?" Zibia asked.

"The Lord made them part. Through me."

"And you really *did* purify the water at Jericho with a handful of salt?"

Again Elisha nodded. "The Lord did. Through me."

"And what of the children of Bethel?" Merari asked the question carefully, not wanting to offend him. Certainly she didn't want to sound as if she questioned the acts of God, but she felt compelled to know whether or not Elisha had, in fact, killed children for jeering at him as she and Nahum had been told. The story worried them. It seemed so unlike Elisha. She exchanged a quick look with Nahum, who gave an almost imperceptible, but approving, nod.

A look of regret crossed Elisha's face.

She felt a sinking feeling inside her. Was the story true, after all?

"You may have offended our guest, my daughter," Zibia reproved.

But Elisha held up a placating hand. "It's all right, little mother. Merari has the right to ask. And you all have the right to know what happened." He shifted uneasily in his chair. "The truth of the matter is this. First, the rumor says I killed children. They were *not* children but young men. Yes, they did jeer at me. Yes, they did call me an old baldhead. Yes, I did curse them. But not for jeering at me, and not for taunting me about my bald head." He made a gesture toward his head and gave a wry smile. "How could I? It's obviously bald. What I did curse them for was their mocking of Jehovah. It was blasphemous. Terrible. Filthy. Yes, I cursed them for that."

"But what about the bears?" Nahum prompted. "The rumors we heard said that you asked God to call forth bears to kill those boys."

Slowly, deliberately, Elisha shook his head. "No one, including me, saw the bears until it was too late. Until some of the young men at the fringe of the crowd already had been mauled. Everyone panicked and scattered. Fled to safety. Including me." The look of regret once more crossed his face. "I didn't stay to defend against the bears. I should have, but I didn't. And many were killed. Or died later."

"I suppose the rumors about it being all your fault could have come from many places," reasoned Zibia. "Even from your servant."

Elisha looked surprised.

"He thinks so highly of you," Zibia went on, "that it might have been his way of lifting you in the sight of others. As another great man of God. So that you would already be equal in stature to Elijah."

The prophet pondered the idea for a long moment. "Gehazi does have an imaginative mind. And a wagging tongue."

Nahum laughed. "What is worse is that he really thinks you are greater than Elijah. That places an awful burden on you, my friend!"

At that they all laughed, and the tension was gone completely. Merari picked up the carafe and refilled their wine cups.

"I doubt that the Lord will ever use me in such great ways as he did Elijah."

"You can never tell," Merari said.

Elisha shook his head. "No. The contest between Elijah and the Baal priests at Mount Carmel will not be equaled by me. Such an event requires a person of greatest faith, Merari."

"That was a wondrous event, all right," Zibia said. "It made true believers of many of us."

"But some people—like Jezebel—thought it was all a trick, didn't they?" Merari asked.

"Yes, my daughter. There were many people, and still are, who judge only from their own point of view."

Elisha leaned toward Zibia. "Were you there, m'lady?"

"Where?"

"At Mount Carmel, when Elijah proved the power of Jehovah."

Zibia nodded.

"Did you see the righteous fire descend from the heavens?"

"I did."

"Would you tell me about it? Elijah spoke only seldom of it."

"I'm sure he told it more eloquently than I could."

"But your view would be somewhat different," Elisha encouraged.

She hesitated, searching his face.

"Tell us, Mother," Merari urged.

"Very well," Zibia agreed, resettling herself in her chair. "It occurred, as I recall, about the time my husband was sent to Jerusalem by King Ahab to attend the coronation of King Jehoshaphat of Judah. Merari was only ten or eleven at the time. I guess you weren't much older, were you, Elisha?"

He nodded in agreement.

"Well, anyway, Merari and her nurse, Achsa, and I came here to stay in Shunem while Benaiah went to Jerusalem. Nahum looked after us." She smiled at him. "I guess that's when we all first became such good friends."

"Why didn't King Ahab go to Jerusalem himself?" Merari asked.

"He was out searching for Elijah."

Elisha laughed in astonishment. "*What?*"

"A great drouth was on the land," Zibia went on. "For more than three years, it had not rained. Things were very bad. Obadiah finally persuaded Ahab that the only way to end the drouth was for him personally to seek out Elijah and to personally ask him to pray to Jehovah for an end to the drouth."

"Ahab begging prayers from Elijah?"

"He was desperate," Zibia explained. "Jezebel's priests had failed to end the drouth. Trade was falling off. Revenues to the king's treasury were reduced. Ben-Hadad of Damascus was threatening the northern border again. Caravans were bypassing us."

"There was no forage for the animals," Nahum remarked. "I can remember that."

"And I even remember how we had to conserve everything in order to share with the villagers," Merari added.

"What happened when Ahab finally found Elijah?"

"He acted like the absolute monarch he was. He ordered Elijah to end the drouth!"

Elisha laughed. It was a compelling laugh, one that shook him from his bald head to his sandals. In fact, it was so infectious that they all joined in.

"Elijah, on the other hand, was in no mood to be ordered about by Ahab," Zibia continued. "He told him that it was his own evil ways causing the drouth in the first place, and that if he wanted it stopped there were certain conditions required of him."

"And one of the conditions was that he gather everyone together at Mount Carmel. Is that right?" asked Elisha.

"That's right. All the people of Israel, plus the 450 Baal priests and the 400 priests of the fertility goddess who were being supported by Jezebel at that time, were to come together at Carmel. When we gathered, Elijah challenged us by saying, If the Lord is God, follow him. But if Baal is God, then follow him.

"And he challenged the priests to see whose god really was the one true God. The test centered around which of the gods could light fires under the sacrificial bullocks on the altars. The Baal priests went first. They prepared their altars and then set about chanting and singing, praying and demanding, in an effort to make their gods respond by setting fires under the altars.

"But there was no response. There was no fire. Then the priests shouted and danced again. Finally they cut themselves with knives and swords until the mountain ran red with their blood. Still there was no answer from their false gods. Then Elijah prepared his altar for the Lord, stood back, looked out across the crowd and began to pray."

Zibia paused. A faraway, reflective look came into her eyes.

"To this very day, I can hear his words of prayer: 'O Lord God of Abraham, Isaac, and Israel, prove today that you are the God of Israel. Answer me so that these people will know that you are God, and that I am your servant, and that you have brought the people back to yourself.' As Elijah finished that prayer, fire as in a lightning bolt flashed down from the heavens. It struck the altar, igniting the wood laid so carefully under the sacrificial bullock. Flames soared, consuming everything, until there was nothing left. And when we, the people, saw it, we fell on our faces to the ground, shouting, "Jehovah is God, Jehovah is God!" "

Elisha sat unmoving, staring at Zibia. He seemed scarcely to breathe. Only his eyes expressed the depth of his feelings. In her deepest heart, Merari realized that she was seeing the power of God moving in her friend, sharing secrets of the power of life with him.

It occurred to her that in her mother's recounting of Elijah's prayer, no mention had been made of the fires from heaven, nor of the drouth. Elijah had simply prayed a prayer of praise, a prayer of confidence in the one true God. He had asked for nothing except that God show himself, in some way, to the people who had strayed from their traditions of moral and spiritual law. Elijah had prayed a prayer of praise. Not a prayer for fire. Not a prayer to end the drouth. The thought struck her hard. It was a concept she had not before imagined, much less reasoned through.

Was there, she now asked herself, a special power in prayers of praise?

Did Elisha, too, know of this power? She seemed to remember his speaking of it. Had she not understood what he really meant? She looked at him.

There were tears in his eyes. With a rough hand, he brushed at them.

"Was it then, my mother, that Elijah prayed for Jehovah to end the drouth?" Merari asked.

Zibia nodded.

"And Jehovah did so?"

"Jehovah did so, my daughter. He sent the rains from the west. Great, dark clouds of rain that moved across the land, soaking the hills, filling the low places, and reviving our spirits. We all had been overtaken by the weariness of drouth's desolation." She turned to Nahum. "You were old enough to remember it, weren't you?"

"Yes. I remember it. Only such a gift of Jehovah's power could have revived us then."

"And what of King Ahab?" Merari asked. "Did it change him at all?"

"Briefly. But it did not last."

"Jezebel's influence of hatred was too great," Nahum said.

With a rueful smile, Zibia agreed. "Jezebel was so furious over the defeat—and eventually the death—of her priests that she set out to have Elijah captured and killed. The Lord protected him, of course, and told him to leave the kingdom. So once more Jezebel was thwarted." She paused. Darkness had fully enveloped the courtyard and servants now brought torches and set them on wall brackets. Zibia continued thoughtfully: "How strange it is, feeling as we do about the Lord God, that your father and I and Obadiah have been allowed to remain a part of the royal court for so long."

The same question often had come into Merari's own mind. The answer, she had supposed, lay in the fact that her parents and Obadiah never openly flaunted their beliefs, never openly opposed the Baal-worship of Jezebel. It was just something else they closed their eyes to.

"It's the power of Jehovah at work," Elisha said. "In every time of evil, the Lord places his people where he needs them. Someday the royal house of this kingdom will be utterly destroyed. The crumbling has already begun. The Lord God already has willed its destruction!"

-3-

Elisha's prophecy of destruction neither angered nor frightened any of them. Perhaps it was because of the influence of Zibia, who habitually took the long-range view of most events, a trait acquired through long years of marriage to a successful diplomat. Or perhaps it was the influence of Nahum's patient acceptance of the cycles in life, which were so like the ever-repeating seasons of nature. Or perhaps, Merari decided later, the prophecy answered some deep need to see an end to the injustices and cruelties perpetrated by the royal house over many generations.

But what seemed most interesting was the fact that, regardless of the reasons for their individual reactions to the prophecy, none of them questioned its truth. Nor did they question Elisha's authority, as a holy man of God, to proclaim such a truth. In fact, they were so convinced of his authority that they discussed ways to nurture his friendship.

"I'm glad we had a place for him to stay," Nahum said the next day after they had bid him good-bye. "Another few days and we would have had no room, what with Athaliah coming and all."

"Athaliah!" Merari exclaimed. "I almost forgot that I had invited her to come for a visit before she and young Ahaziah return to Jerusalem."

"Forgot? How could you?" asked Nahum.

"She's not bringing that boy with her, I hope." Zibia cut in.

"Yes, she is bringing the boy. At least, I invited her to."

"It's all right, Zibia," Nahum said reassuringly. "I'll see

that the boy is entertained and kept out of your way. What worries me is Merari's memory."

"There's nothing wrong with my memory."

"I'm not so certain of that. What if Elisha had come a few days later? Where would we have housed him?"

"I don't know," she said defensively. "Perhaps we should have a special room built for him."

Zibia and Nahum looked at each other in surprise.

"Well, after all, he said he would be coming and going often between the prophets' school on Mount Carmel and the capital city."

"A special room for Elisha?" Nahum said in a tone of consideration. "That really is quite a hospitable idea, Merari. I like it."

"Ideally, it should be a quiet place where he could be alone to pray and meditate. But where would we find such a spot in this house?" Zibia asked.

"Maybe we could build a room on the wall itself," Nahum suggested. "Then he would have peace and quiet and be out of the house. We'll talk more about it later."

But, it would be weeks before they once more would speak about it. On the second day after Elisha's departure, Benaiah arrived from Samaria with Athaliah and her son and a retinue of servants. The trip had not been an easy one.

"Athaliah has changed even more for the worse," Benaiah reported to them privately. "She's not the lively, chattering young woman I remember."

"She has been a Judean princess for some years now, my father."

"But must it sit so heavily on her? She reminds me more and more of Jezebel. Complaining, manipulating, demanding."

"What about the boy?" Nahum asked.

"A brat. An impossible brat!"

In the ensuing days, the household came to understand how right Benaiah was. Merari's anticipation of a fine reunion with Athaliah went unfulfilled. Athaliah slept late, ate most meals in her rooms, left the supervision of ten-year-old Ahaziah to the servants, and generally kept to herself. On the few occasions when she did appear, she was pleasant enough on the surface, but noticeably uninterested and preoccupied. Merari decided that her girlhood friend was exhausted from all the rituals and the festivities required of her in the aftermath of Joram's coronation.

Meanwhile, Nahum and Merari tried to befriend Ahaziah. The eldest of six sons born to Athaliah and Jehoram of Judah, he was his mother's favorite. Unfortunately, he was keenly aware of that fact. His manners were bad, and he resisted all efforts at friendship.

"I don't understand it," Nahum puzzled. "All children like you, beloved. I have seen babies stop crying when you pick them up and hold them. Most children Ahaziah's age follow you around and want to be near you. But this lad . . ."

She gave a rueful smile. "We must keep on trying. Take him into the fields with you. Maybe that will interest him."

He did as she asked. He gave the lad a horse to ride; took him into the fields and orchards, and had Kallai fashion a sling and teach him how to track and hunt hares with it. The boy, however, found the fields and the orchards boring. He complained loudly and constantly about the heat and the dust. He had no patience for hunting hares; instead, he turned the sling toward human targets with an almost diabolic glee.

"They're only slaves," he declared, when told to stop.

"Not in Shunem," Kallai warned. "These are free people, as free as you. But even if they weren't, you don't use slings against people. Stop it!"

"You can't talk to me that way. I am a Prince of Judah. I can do as I wish!"

"Not on these lands, young donkey." Kallai grabbed the sling, threw it away, and carried the screaming, struggling boy back to the house to his mother.

It was this incident that finally brought Athaliah out of

her rooms, dismayed and searching for Merari. She found her in the pottery shed with Tamar, checking the stock of new jars made for the oil from the forthcoming olive harvest. "Great stars!" Athaliah exclaimed, coming into the shed. "Who would ever need this many pots and jars on a farm?"

Merari and Tamar turned in surprise.

"I'm serious, Merari. How can you possibly use all of these? I doubt we have this many in the palace in Jerusalem. There must be hundreds here!"

Tamar looked astonished. Athaliah's ignorance of the working world of a farm was obvious. But how could it be otherwise? All she knew was palace life. Why should she be expected to know anything at all about a farm?

"We'll begin harvesting olives soon. The jars will be used for the crop. Some will be used for the new wine, too, when we harvest grapes later on."

Athaliah slowly walked down the length of the shed, looking at the jars. "Did you help make these jars?"

Merari followed along behind her friend. "Yes, I helped to make some of them." She traced a finger down the curving fullness of one of the jars. The clay was cool to the touch, and beckoning her to work again at the potter's wheel. Pottery was a craft she had learned in childhood and had always loved. Recently, there had been no time for it. But maybe later. After harvest. After all the company of visitors had left. Maybe then.

Athaliah stopped, turned, and gave her a direct look. "I shall certainly have to keep Ahaziah and his sling out of here, won't I?"

The abrupt, roundabout apology caught Merari by surprise.

Then, from behind her, Tamar snickered.

Athaliah's face reddened.

Merari motioned for the servant to leave.

"I *shall* keep him out of here," Athaliah stoutly declared. "After all, I certainly don't want him destroying the whole place. It's dreadful what he did! Great stars, who would think little Ahaziah would stone a person?"

Merari waited.

Athaliah's dark eyes widened until they dominated her thin face. She glanced past Merari's shoulder to make sure the servant Tamar was gone. "Do you know what my son told me when I asked him why he did such a dreadful thing?"

"What?"

"He told me that if King David could do it to a Philistine, he could use a sling against an Israelite, because someday he, too, would be a king!"

Merari stared in astonishment.

"Can you imagine it? It's very like something my dear mother, Jezebel, might have taught him. Can you imagine?"

Yes, Merari thought to herself, she could imagine it. It was typical for members of the royal house to excuse their meanness and their cruelty as a privilege of royal authority. Yes, she could imagine it.

"I'd hate to think my son considers you and your people the enemy just because you live in the Northern Kingdom." The stricken look on Athaliah's face appeared genuine. "You don't suppose my son really thinks that, do you?"

The whole situation suddenly seemed funny. Ridiculous, in fact. Merari began to laugh.

Puzzled, then indignant, Athaliah drew back. You're making fun of me!"

"No," she gasped through her laughter.

"Oh, yes you are, Merari! You're making fun of me. Just like you always did!"

Merari denied it again with a shake of her head.

Petulance got the best of Athaliah and brought with it a hard, spiteful backbiting. "If you had a son, you'd be more understanding!"

Laugher fled. Merari tensed.

Athaliah's eyes flashed. "You have no children, so you

don't know what it's like to raise one up. Yet you make fun of me!"

"Should I apologize?"

"You should've married Joram! That's what you should've done."

Anger coursed through Merari. She fought it down. "That's uncalled for!"

"Well, you *should* have." Athaliah walked away a few steps, her shoulders rigid. "If you had married Joram, you could've had children! But instead, you married an old farmer and—"

"Enough, Athaliah!"

"Well, it's true, Merari. You didn't have to marry a man so much older, and only a farmer, at that. Joram was right when he said that to you at his coronation."

Anger shot through Merari afresh. This time she didn't bridle it. "I said, that's enough! You're a guest in this house. In the house of the old farmer. We welcome you. Both the old farmer and his wife. But such words are not welcome. Now or ever."

Athaliah's mouth gaped open in astonishment.

"We've been friends too long to be this unkind to each other, Athaliah." Merari went to her. "But I cannot let you talk about Nahum like that. And I won't!"

Athaliah stood her ground, but glanced away.

"We both carry heavy burdens. Even though they are not the same kind of burdens, we must respect each other, if nothing else."

Athaliah relented. "I owe you another apology, don't I?"

"Just don't say those things. Not here. And not to me."

Athaliah faltered. "Why is it you're always right, and I'm always wrong?"

"Does it matter?"

"To me, it does."

"And it matters to me, too!" boomed a man's voice from behind them.

Astonished, both turned.

Joram stood in the doorway watching them. He was dressed in the uniform of a charioteer. The short black tunic and wrought-silver breastplate were covered with the dust of the road. He ran one hand through his dark, thick hair and a small shower of dust cascaded onto his broad shoulders.

The slightest shiver of fear went through Merari.

"How long have you been standing there?" demanded Athaliah.

"Long enough, my vixen of a sister." He gave a hard laugh.

She walked toward him. "What are you doing here? I don't remember Merari inviting you."

"I came to see you, Honorable Princess of Judah." He gave a swashbuckling, comedic bow from the waist.

"You must want something," she snapped.

"I do. There's state business which must be discussed with you."

"What kind of state business?"

"It's to be discussed with Benaiah, as well, so be patient, my sister." He brushed past her and went to Merari. "In all truth, there is a matter of greatest urgency I must discuss with your father. Is he here?" An expression of genuine worry filled his eyes.

"He is here."

"Will you take me to him?"

She nodded and moved toward the doorway; then hesitated and stepped aside to let Joram and Athaliah go out before her. It was a matter of royal protocol, a habit not easily broken.

Outside the pottery shed, Commander Jehu, King's Adjutant, stood waiting. Tamar and two other of the household servants were nearby. At the appearance of Joram, all the servants bowed low. Jehu salaamed. Merari instructed Tamar to lead the royal guests into the main salon of the house while she went to find her father.

As she turned to go, Jehu saluted her and handed her a

small leather message pouch. "If you will, please give this to your father. The Honorable Obadiah asked that I bring it."

Merari nodded, took the pouch, and went to find her father.

As it turned out, the urgent matter that had brought Joram to Shunem so unexpectedly was a problem with Mesha, King of Moab, who had grown weary of paying an annual tribute to Israel. His people were sheepherders. Their annual tribute to Israel amounted to one hundred thousand lambs and the wool from one hundred thousand rams. What they received from Israel in return was a protected border and men-at-arms in the event they were set upon by mutual enemies. This arrangement had been negotiated during the reign of King Ahab years before by Benaiah. Now, because of an affront by Jezebel and Joram's late brother, Ahaziah, Mesha had decided to pay no more tribute.

Instead, he sent a declaration of independence to Joram's royal court. The declaration stated, in effect, that since Mesha now considered Moab an independent nation, he no longer needed nor wanted Israel's protection for its borders, and therefore Moab would no longer pay tribute to Israel. It was the receipt of this communication which had brought Joram unannounced to Shunem to seek Benaiah's advice.

"I agree with you, sire. It is a gravely serious matter." Benaiah indicated a chair for the king with customary courtesy.

Joram declined with a shake of his head, forcing everyone else to remain standing. Everyone except Athaliah. She sank down on a gilt settee of Philistine design.

"Are there refreshments for our guests, Merari?" Benaiah asked.

"I shall see to them at once." She turned, grateful for the chance to get away from Joram.

But he stopped her. "There will be no time for refresh-

ments. Jehu and I have business yet this day at Megiddo."
She returned to stand near Athaliah.

Joram pulled a sheepskin scroll from his vestment, unrolled it, and handed it to Benaiah. "You know Mesha personally, and rather well, don't you?"

"Yes, I know him. Your father promoted him to Royal Sheepmaster some years ago. Then, when your father was killed in battle at Ramoth-Gilead, Mesha named himself King of Moab."

"Do you think this declaration is valid? Does Mesha mean what this says?"

Benaiah read the scroll and looked up with a frown. "It is valid, my king. This is Mesha's seal. It is written as he would speak it. He means it. He intends to pay Israel no more tribute."

"Then it is not just a bluff? To test a new, young king?"

Respect glimmered for an instant in the older man's eyes. He rerolled the scroll and handed it back. "I think not, m'lord. I believe you can now consider Moab our enemy."

Joram cursed and turned away.

Jehu spoke up in a deep and rumbling voice. "But sire, why do we worry? We have men, and we have the arms, and we—"

"It's too soon for a war, Jehu!" Joram interrupted, pacing away and rubbing his hands together.

The words had blazed from Joram in such anger that Athaliah threw a nervous look toward Merari. Joram never backed away from fights unless he thought he couldn't win.

Benaiah, face expressionless, folded his arms across his chest and began to rock back and forth on his heels, playing for time, suspecting that something more was on Joram's mind and waiting for him to reveal it.

Jehu shifted his weight from one foot to the other and adjusted the short dagger at his waist. Athaliah kept a steady gaze directed at her brother. And Merari watched her father.

Joram continued to pace but said nothing more.

Finally, Benaiah asked, "Is it that you expect a trap, m'lord?"

Joram turned. "Exactly."

Jehu's eyes widened.

Athaliah flinched.

"Do you expect that the trap will come from the King of Syria?" Benaiah asked.

Joram nodded.

Benaiah gave a tentative shrug. "It's possible, I suppose. But rather unlikely, I think."

"Oh? Why unlikely?"

"Unlikely because Ben-Hadad of Damascus has been very troublesome for the King of Syria lately. He's like some nettlesome fly that avoids being swatted."

Joram's laugh sounded hollow. "But suppose this fly already has been swatted? Just in recent days. And suppose that the King of Syria now has turned his attention and his favor toward Moab's rebellion against us? What then?"

Benaiah stopped rocking back and forth on his heels. A frown creased his face. "We would be in a full-fledged war with Syria. We would be outnumbered, sire, and we might suffer a defeat. Unless, of course, we could call on an ally."

A smile of agreement spread across Joram's dark face. "And which ally would that be?"

"A strong ally, I should think, sire," Benaiah said. "An ally who is very close to us."

Joram's glance slid toward Athaliah.

Instantly, she was on her feet. "So *that's* it! That's what you want of me?"

"That's it, my sister." He walked toward her. "I want the armies of Jehoshaphat of Judah."

"You're mad!"

"I want Jehoshaphat's armies," he repeated. "I want Jehoshaphat as an ally. I want his help in putting down Moab's rebellion."

"And you want me to tell that to Jehoshaphat?"

Joram shook his head condescendingly. "Not tell. Ask, my sister. Ask. I want you to *ask* Jehoshaphat to commit his armies to me."

"Ask him yourself!" she said bitterly and walked toward the far side of the room.

Joram followed. "He's not *my* father-in-law."

"That makes no difference."

"It could."

"I have no special influence with him. How could I persuade him?"

Joram moved closer to her. "You have more influence than you know."

She pushed him away and turned her back.

"He sent you to my coronation. As his personal representative. He sent you instead of his own son! Obviously, he must respect you. Obviously, he trusts you."

"Use your head," she snapped, turning on him. "He sent me because I'm your sister, and because he hates our mother. He hates her so much that he doesn't want his own son—my husband—in this kingdom!"

But Joram persisted. "Your father-in-law will do this for you. You have borne him six grandsons. I will bet my favorite racing chariot on it. He trusts you."

A strange, calculating light crept into her eyes. Still she hesitated.

Joram shrugged, and in his gesture was a vulnerable quality. "If I ask him, he'll turn me down. Just as he turned down our brother's request for help to re-establish the old trade routes to Ezion-Geber."

"That was different," Athaliah said. "Those old trade routes cut right through the heart of Judah. Jehoshaphat was afraid our mother would promote the capture of all Judah's border fortresses. And she would have. But this . . ."

Now it was Joram who turned away, feigning disappointment, playing for time.

"The king is right about Jehoshaphat's respect for you, Your Highness," Benaiah said to Athaliah. "There's no doubt that your asking him to help us would result in his support."

Athaliah acknowledged his comment with a slight smile.

Joram remained perfectly still, as if any motion on his part would cause Athaliah to refuse him out of spite. Into Merari's mind flashed a hundred similar incidents from childhood when, in fact, Athaliah had done just that. The irony almost overwhelmed her. Had they all changed so little?

"Putting down Moab's rebellion is as important to Judah as to Israel," Benaiah pointed out matter-of-factly.

New interest flickered in Athaliah's eyes. "Yes, it is, isn't it?"

"Absolutely."

"I can see that clearly. And it would be bad for both kingdoms if . . ." Her voice trailed away. Quiet crept over the room.

"Moab's rebellion could be disastrous, Your Highness," Benaiah softly prompted.

Athaliah straightened and turned to Joram. "All right, my brother."

He wheeled around, a broad smile on his face.

"I will do as you ask. On one condition."

He stopped. "What condition?"

"Benaiah must go with me to Jerusalem as your personal representative. Jehoshaphat will believe him."

"Very well," Joram agreed.

"And there is something else, too."

"What?"

"You said earlier that you were going to Megiddo, didn't you?"

"I did."

"How long will you stay?"

"One, two days, maybe. Why?"

"I want you to take your nephew, Ahaziah, with you."

The request was so out of context that it astonished them all.

Jehu was plainly stunned; Benaiah simply looked puzzled.

A sense of relief swept through Merari. Nahum and Kallai would be jubilant if this should happen!

Joram, however, was far from jubilant. A heavy frown creased the space between his eyes. Anger edged into his face. "By the eyes of Baal, Athaliah! Have you lost your senses?"

She walked slowly back to the gilt settee without answering and sat down.

"What has this to do with what we have been talking about?" Joram demanded.

"A great deal, if you think about it."

"Explain it to me."

"It's really quite simple. Young Ahaziah is the apple of his grandfather's eye. Can you imagine the effect on Jehoshaphat when the bright ten-year-old tells him about the strength and the power of Israel's chariot corps from Megiddo, which his Uncle Joram took him to see? Can you picture the impact this could have on your request for an alliance to put down Moab's rebellion?"

For the second time in as many minutes, an astonished silence swept over the gathering. Athaliah was, indeed, her mother's own daughter, Merari decided. Jezebel herself could not have been more shrewd. From the looks on the faces of the men in the room, that fact was not lost on them, either.

"But, I must warn you, my brother," Athaliah went on. "My eldest son will be impressed by everything you say and by everything you do." She cast a surreptitious glance at Merari and a grin crinkled at the corner of her mouth. "My child will be impressed with your every action, because you are a king," she concluded, turning again to Joram. "In spite of yourself, you are a king. You will be his example because, as he so recently told me, he, too, will someday be a king."

-4-

In the immediate aftermath of Joram's visit, Athaliah returned to the seclusion of her rooms. Benaiah called his scribe and set about preparing documents for the trip to Jerusalem. Zibia retired for the night, upset that Benaiah would be traveling again so soon. And Nahum closeted himself in the small office at one end of the pottery shed to go over records of the day's harvesting.

The house was quiet. Merari wandered about enjoying being alone. She welcomed the chance to sort out some things that disturbed her about Joram's visit. She pulled a shawl from a nearby chest, shrugged it over her shoulders, and stepped out into the courtyard. The canopy of night was interrupted by star-sprinklings of diamond lights. Softly beckoning her to calm ponderings and meditation, the troublesome thoughts could be sorted, and put in perspective, and perhaps even conquered, if she tried very hard, she told herself.

She pulled the shawl closer, warding off the coolness of the night air, and began to walk. Three things bothered her. The first was the fact that no mention had been made of Nahum's reappointment as Royal Overseer. More than enough time had passed for Joram to have acted officially on the reappointment. But Nahum's name had not even been mentioned during the visit—except, of course, for Athaliah's hurtful reference just before Joram arrived.

And that led to the second troublesome thought. "An old farmer who can give you no children," Athaliah had said scornfully. How unfair! The fact that Athaliah had borne six children gave her no right to be scornful of someone who could have none. How unfair indeed! If she let herself dwell on it, she could weep the most bitter of tears, as she had done during the early years of marriage. Then there had been teasing from Uncle Obadiah, pressure from her family and from friends who were having babies. *Everyone* was having babies, except for them. It was as if she and Nahum were outcasts. The passing years had only magnified her longings for a child, served to heighten her yearning to hold a precious child of her own in her arms, to suckle and nourish, cuddle and cherish her own baby.

Tears welled up, blurring the starlit courtyard and forcing her to a standstill. She trembled against memory's tension. "Stop it," she told herself sternly. "You have a good life with Nahum. Child or no child, you have no reason to feel sorry for yourself. All is well." She brushed the tears away with the tips of her fingers. Regardless of Athaliah's scorn, or anyone else's, she must not give way like this again. She simply must not.

The courtyard gradually came back into focus. She readjusted her shawl and began to retrace her steps. There was yet a third thing troubling her. Joram. Joram himself. He had exhibited a facet of his personality that she had never seen before: the force and authority of leadership. She found the quality admirable, and the very idea that she could admire anything about Joram disturbed her. She long since had come to terms about Joram. Or so she thought. As long as she regarded him with total dislike and total mistrust, her required reaction to him was avoidance. But during today's unprecedented visit, she had seen something in him which she not only admired, but which caused a revival of feelings much too lenient. Even compromising, perhaps. Certainly contradictory. It all seemed disloyal, somehow, to Nahum. Dear Nahum.

She crossed out of the courtyard, passed through a side exit of the house, and made her way toward the small office in the pottery shed. Nahum was seated on a bench at a crudely made desk. Light from two small lamps burnished his weather-tanned face and outlined the strength of his brow.

Painstakingly, he rechecked the weights and measures which Kallai had marked on the papyrus scroll earlier in the day, while they were still in the fields. No other Royal Overseer was as scrupulous with record-keeping. Nor could any other in the kingdom equal Nahum in coaxing heavy yields from the stubborn land. If for no other reason, thought Merari, Joram should need no coaxing to reappoint him. Dear Nahum.

She went to him and placed her arms about his shoulders, leaned down to press her face close to his. The clean smell of earth was still on him. The texture of his homespun tunic felt rough and sturdy against her forearms, matching her perception of his stability and eternal protectiveness.

He turned his head ever so slightly, returning her gesture of affection. "Are you restless after all the excitement of this afternoon?"

"In a way, I suppose."

"You should be. It isn't every day a king comes to a farmer's house."

She swiveled about and sank down next to him on the bench. "Why do you suppose he's taking so long to reappoint you?"

Nahum shrugged. "The press of other affairs, I suspect. At least that's what Benaiah and Obadiah think."

She shook her head. "Then why can't *I* believe that? Why do I so frequently imagine there are other reasons?"

"I don't know, beloved." He sighed heavily. "Maybe it's because you're right. I hope not. But maybe it is." He turned again to his accounting.

For several minutes, she considered it all again, staring into the dark spaces beyond the lamplight. Logically, there was no reason to think that Joram's delay was caused by anything other than more pressing affairs. Certainly the Moab situation *was* pressing. And yet something other than logic pushed at her from the shadowy fringe of her mind.

"Naboth's vineyard." She said the words out loud, but unexpectedly, and in such hushed tones that for an instant she didn't realize they were her words.

"What did you say?" Nahum asked, looking at her in surprise.

"Naboth's vineyard," she repeated.

"What about it?"

"Do you remember the story about it?"

"Who doesn't? It was the act that brought the wrath of God down on this land. But it was Jezebel who did that awful thing. What has that do with us?"

"You remember how she did it?"

Nahum put the accounts aside and thought for a moment. "Let's see. Naboth was a man who believed in Jehovah. But Jezebel *falsely* accused him of cursing God. Then she falsely accused him of cursing King Ahab. She bought off two witnesses to swear Naboth had done these things. In the end, she demanded that, according to the law, the good citizens of Jezreel should stone Naboth to death! And they did it."

Merari nodded. "But do you remember *why* she did it?"

"Because Naboth wouldn't sell his vineyard to Ahab."

She gripped his arm. "Oh, Nahum, Joram may be no better than his mother when it comes to taking what he wants now that he's king!"

Nahum put his arm around her and pulled her close. "Joram cannot harm us. He cannot take you from me. He cannot take our lands. There are now new laws in the kingdom. Benaiah and Obadiah have seen to that. Joram will take his time about my reappointment. He will taunt us with it, because it gives him pleasure to worry you. But he is not Jezebel."

She sighed. "Perhaps this is another of those times when I should say, 'All is well,' even though I really don't think so."

He released her with a chuckle. "And perhaps this is one of those times when we should leave these accountings and go into the house for supper. Your imagination always runs away with you when you are hungry."

In the family's private portion of the house, they found Benaiah pacing back and forth, still dictating to his scribe. Rolls of papyrus and writing-skins lay on the floor beside the writing table in an abandoned heap. From the number of them, two things could be assumed: Benaiah was having one of his rare moments when the proper turn of phrase escaped him; or there were many different messages to many different people already completed.

Beyond, at the far end of the room, a long table was still set with a variety of foods. Meats, fruits, vegetables, cheeses. An enormous loaf of bread with bits broken off one end sat beside a flagon of wine and the drinking cups. Merari and Nahum made their way toward the table. Benaiah stopped dictating to look up and wave to them, then stooped over his scribe's shoulder to recheck his last words.

"That will do." He clapped the scribe on the shoulder. "See that all these are carefully packed for the trip. You will come with me. We leave tomorrow, provided King Joram has returned early enough in the day from Megiddo with young Ahaziah."

The scribe nodded, got to his feet and bowed to them all, gathered up the heap of scrolls from the floor, and vanished through the gallery archway. Benaiah joined Merari and Nahum at the food table. "Your mother has decided to come with me to Jerusalem, Merari. She will visit there a few days and then go on to Joppa with me. We will visit your Aunt Ilia, and I will conduct some business with the King of Philistia. I wish you would come, too."

"The trip would do you good," Nahum urged.

She reached for a bit of bread. "There's too much to be done here; I couldn't leave now."

"But the grain harvest is almost finished." Nahum reminded her. "And it will be several weeks yet before the olive and grape harvests start."

"Until then, Nahum can manage without you," her father encouraged.

"Perhaps it is that I cannot manage without him, my father." She moved down the food table and picked up a bit of cheese. "Besides, there's the room for Elisha to be readied."

"That can wait," Nahum said. "The trip will help you get your mind off your worries."

"What worries?" Benaiah asked.

"She worries over my reappointment from Joram. Or rather, the lack of it."

"Oh, yes." Benaiah reached into his vestment and pulled out the small leather message pouch that Jehu earlier had asked Merari to give to him. "I forgot about having this until now. It's from Obadiah. Perhaps about your reappointment, Nahum." He opened the pouch, pulled forth and unfolded a small writing-skin, and quickly scanned its contents. With a shake of his head, he glanced at them. "It says nothing about your reappointment. It only reminds me to prepare documents to be sent to Edom. If Joram agrees, of course. Edom, too, will be an important ally in the fight against Moab." He refolded the writing-skin, put it back into the leather pouch, and stuffed the pouch back into his vestment.

Merari frowned.

"It is as I said earlier," Nahum reminded her, "Joram has a war on his mind. There is nothing sinister about his delay in reappointing me."

"You really feel that all is well?" she asked.

He nodded.

"And I agree, my child," her father confirmed. "Now come, let us eat and then retire. Remember, tomorrow will be a long day for your father. I shall be traveling again with Queen Athaliah and that son of hers."

Quite early the next day, Joram and Jehu returned from Megiddo. They tarried at the house in Shunem only long enough to deposit Ahaziah with Athaliah and to go over last-minute details with Benaiah about military rendezvous points, troop movements, and lines of supply and communications. All agreed that in the interest of security and secrecy, trusted servants should be used as couriers, rather than those from the royal court. Joram's manservant, Manoah, would be dispatched from Samaria to meet Benaiah in Jerusalem and carry word of Jehoshaphat's decision back to Joram. Shual, manservant to Obadiah, would be entrusted to carry a message directly to the King of Edom, requesting passage for Israel's and Judah's armies through the wilderness area of his kingdom on Moab's southern border.

"That permit to pass through Edom is of greatest importance," Joram said to Benaiah, as he and Jehu prepared to leave the compound once again. "It will allow me easier entry into Mesha's territory."

"The plan is a good one." Benaiah agreed, bidding them farewell. "God go with you." The phrase had slipped out. Benaiah flushed.

Joram smirked, clicked to his horses, and drove off.

Jehu, on the other hand, saluted Benaiah. "And may the Lord God Jehovah smile on your mission to Jerusalem, sir!"

Within another hour, the caravan from Jerusalem was on its way out of the compound, carrying Athaliah, Ahaziah, and their retinue of servants, Zibia, Benaiah, and assorted aides. Merari and Nahum watched the caravan grow smaller and smaller across the distance of the Plain of Jezreel. As they turned back, Nahum kissed her and went off toward the tannery. Merari went toward the house, realizing that for the first time in many weeks, it was now empty of guests. No more were expected for a time. Calm and quiet would finally hold forth.

There would be time to reflect on all the recent happenings and put them into proper perspective. There would be more time alone with Nahum, too; to walk hand-in-hand in the soft dusk of evening, to share the laughter of their love, and to lie together in the deep, rhythmic silences of the night. How wonderful it would be, she thought, if such a quiet time of renewal finally would bring a child into their lives.

For three days, the idyllic quiet she dreamed of actually existed. The rest was wonderful. Tamar even quit fussing about missing Gehazi. But it was too good to last. On the fourth day, the house in Shunem once more was playing host to a series of guests. A merchant from Joppa arrived to contract with Nahum for a shipment of barley and new oil. A husbandman from Endor came down to arrange for his cattle to forage on the freshly harvested fields. A weaver and his three sons from the Galilee hills wandered by, selling robes of beautiful homespun. They brought with them reports that Joram's men were going about everywhere in the kingdom, numbering the people in preparation for a war with Moab.

And then Elisha came again for a visit! He arrived in the heat of midday, accompanied by Gehazi, who immediately vanished in search of Tamar.

"My visit must be a short one," Elisha explained to Merari, as they walked through the outer gate toward the house. He seemed worried, preoccupied. "I'm on my way back to Samaria from Mount Carmel."

"I will send for Nahum," Merari said. "He's just over in the west vineyard. He'll want to see you."

"No, don't disturb him. I can only stay for a very short time."

"At least stay long enough for some food and a cooling drink," Merari urged.

"You're a lady of great hospitality." Beads of perspiration glistened on his bald head like some evanescent crown. From the folds of his tunic, he retrieved a small square of cotton fabric and mopped at them. Merari sent a servant to fetch refreshments and led him to the coolest part of the courtyard.

"I hope that all is well with you, Elisha. You seem preoccupied."

A frown of concern settled onto his face. "I am, I suppose. I keep hearing rumors of war with Moab. Are the rumors I hear true?"

"Yes, they're true."

He pounded his fist into his palm in disapproval. "War settles nothing!" A servant came from the back of the house with pitchers of water and cool, fresh milk. He took water first, drank it down, and with a heavy sigh stared across the courtyard in silence.

Merari began to tell him of Joram's visit, and of her father's mission to Jerusalem seeking the alliance with King Jehoshaphat. "All of this happened many days past, of course. I suppose by now the alliance has been sealed and the armies are mustering."

Elisha tensed. "Jehoshaphat wouldn't do that. Surely he wouldn't. Not an alliance with Joram the jackal! It cannot be. It *must* not be." He sat rigid in his chair. His face was frightening; his eyes took on a fanatical fire. He got to his feet, paced away a few steps, and returned. "Jehoshaphat is God's man. Joram is Baal's man—and son of that infamous Jezebel. There must be no alliance." He fairly shouted the words and again pounded his fist into his palm. "There must be no alliance!"

Involuntarily, Merari backed away from him.

Elisha turned and went toward the long gallery leading to the back of the house and yelled for Gehazi. Within seconds, the servant came into view. Tamar trailed after him.

"Master? You need me?" The servant's eyes, always protruding, seemed now to bulge frog-like in their sockets. "Are you sick?"

"Yes. Sick of evil at every hand. We must go."

Merari went to him. "But what can you do, my friend?"

"I can stop this unholy alliance from taking place. That's what I can do."

"But how? My father left days ago. The alliance is no doubt already sealed."

He refused her logic with a shake of his head. "No. Jehoshaphat will listen to me. I will go to Jerusalem to talk with him."

Gehazi shot a quick, disappointed look in Tamar's direction.

"But you cannot get there in time, Elisha," Merari insisted. "My father and the others have been there many days now."

Elisha stood motionless, as if listening for something from a great distance. A strange, glazed look appeared in his eyes.

Curious at the noisy outburst of a few moments earlier, several servants had come into the gallery and were staring openly at the holy man. Merari noticed and motioned for them to go away. Then she went to Elisha and put her hand on his arm. "If you insist on going to Jerusalem, at least let me give you and Gehazi horses. It will make your journey faster."

He turned, looked at her unseeing, then blinked several times until his eyes once more held their normal expression. "I'm sorry, Merari. What did you say?"

"At least let me give you horses to make your journey faster. It will take only a short time to make them ready. And Nahum will never forgive me if I don't insist that you take them for yourself and for Gehazi."

The servant looked hopeful. "Take the horses, master. Remember your feet. And those of your poor servant, as well."

With a nod, Elisha agreed.

Merari sent Tamar and Gehazi to find the grooms and make ready the horses, while she encouraged Elisha to sit back down.

Reluctantly, he did so.

"You once told me, Elisha, that threats from forces outside the kingdom should be resisted by all of us. Baal worshipers and Jehovah worshipers alike."

He glanced sharply at her.

"Have you changed your mind about that just because Joram is now king?" she asked.

"You're a bold woman, Merari."

"I'm my father's own daughter," she said calmly, surprised at her boldness but refusing to back away. "He and my mother used to tell me about the boldness of Elijah in times of outside threats. He would go right into the palace to confront Ahab and give him counsel, even in the face of all the danger represented by Jezebel and her priests. Only one time did he not do that: when the Lord warned him in a dream to seek sanctuary outside the kingdom. Elijah obeyed the Lord. He always did, didn't he?"

Elisha frowned.

"Has the Lord told you to stop the alliance between Israel and Judah? Has the Lord told you He wants Moab to be victorious over this kingdom?"

Elisha glanced away.

From the gallery, Tamar signaled that the horses were ready.

"You have much more wisdom than I, old friend," Merari added, standing up. "Maybe your journey to see King Jehoshaphat is the will of the Lord. Besides, I have no right to talk to you this way. You're right; I *have* been bold."

"Indeed you have, Merari of Shunem. Indeed you have." He stood up and smiled at her.

-5-

The combined armies of Israel and Judah made a sizable host. This host included foot soldiers with lances and spears, shield bearers, archers, men with slings and stones, charioteers, and sundry servants, lackeys, and grooms. In addition, there were supply trains of camels and donkeys burdened with tents and tools, waterskins and foodstuffs; and drovers and herdsmen with the cattle and goats which provided fresh meat and fresh milk for the host.

The two armies rendezvoused just below Jericho at the northwestern tip of the Dead Sea. Joram's men funneled down from the Northern Kingdom into the palm-studded Plain of Jericho, while most of Jehoshaphat's men came across the old Jericho road from Jerusalem. Others, stationed at Gerar and Beersheba, filtered across the wilderness of Judah to meet them later.

From the rendezvous point, they trailed south along the western shore of the Dead Sea. Except for the springs at EnGedi halfway down its length, the country they traveled through was waterless and scorched by a merciless sun. The expanse of water constantly at their left was briny and undrinkable. Its sulphurous smell made it unbearable for bathing. Men and animals quickly parched. The pace of travel was slow. At the southern end of the Dead Sea, they turned eastward through the Valley of Salt; and within another day's journey, they reached the place where the River Zered emptied into the southeastern edge of the Dead Sea.

This circuitous route had taken five days of hard travel. Two more days' journey lay ahead before they would engage the enemy. But here, in a brief flood plain, they encamped to rest and refresh themselves and to rendezvous with the forces of the King of Edom. It was an ideal place for an encampment; for it was at this point where the Zered spread out and coursed through a broad plain stretching eastward for two miles or more. Willows, green and sheer, laced Zered's banks with shade. Pastures, green and lush, gave a welcome break to the spirits of the men and to the bellies of the animals from the harsh landscape through which they had just traveled. At its eastern edge, the plain abruptly gave way to a forbidding escarpment of a great canyon carved by the ancient Zered, and created a natural barrier between Edom on the south and Moab on the north. Only many miles further yet to the east did the land and the river once again come together at the same general level and make a fording place on the King's Highway at Aineh.

In the canyon itself, marl, basalt and sandstone—yellow, gray-black, and red—layered the sheer, steep walls. Natural sculptures in stone, weird and majestic, thrust skyward out of the gray-blacks and the reds as if daring the gods of nature to topple them into the abyss. Minarets of yellow marl mimicked the fantasy forms of dreams; and beneath them all ran the river. Unpredictable. Now a trickle. Then, without warning, a tumult. Unlike the Jordan, which had a known flood season from the snowmelt of the northern mountains, the Zered waxed and waned capriciously. It received the drainage from all the tributaries in all of Edom and Moab. It was unpredictable, tenacious; like the people who lived in the nations it divided.

When the armies of Israel, Judah, and Edom finally moved forward once more, they climbed up from the Zered's green floodplain to a plateau, brown and sere, which flanked the canyon on Edom's side. Once again, the country was waterless. Great clouds of yellowish dust kicked up by the host hovered above men and animals, suspended in the sullen, fetid air, and marked their advance.

North, across Zered's gorge, Moabites watched from

precipitous fortresses. With small squares of burnished copper, they flashed reports about the advancing host to other strongholds. From one fortress to another, the message was relayed until it reached King Mesha of Moab at Aineh. Nor were the Moabites the only ones using the great dust clouds to mark the location and movement of the armies.

Elisha and Gehazi, too, were watching. Less than half a day's journey behind the host, they trailed along at a leisurely pace. There was no longer a need to hurry. The alliance had been cast. It was too late to stop it. Instead, Elisha had decided this was the time to call on the graciousness of the one true God for a victory for Israel and Judah and Edom over Moab. The great prophet Elijah would have done the same, as Merari had reminded him so boldly.

"When we fight among ourselves," Elijah had often told him, "I pray for and fight with those who believe in Jehovah. But when we are threatened from beyond our borders, I pray for and fight with all our people, whether or not they are believers. You must learn to do the same. The unity of Israel and Judah must come again someday. That, too, is the will of God."

And so for the next two days, Elisha and Gehazi trailed after the three armies of Israel, Judah, and Edom, and waited for the proper moment to be of help.

On the third day, the fording place at the King's Highway near Aineh was reached. Once more, the armies encamped beside the River Zered, where they had expected to find plenty of water. But only a trickle meandered down the waterway and over the stones that marked the fording place.

The cattle and goats, a-thirst from the arid journey, smelled the water, little as there was, and stampeded to get to it. Bellowing and bleating, they clustered and jostled about the riverbed, muddying the meandering trickle and making it undrinkable for the soldiers. Some of the cattle sank belly-deep in quicksand. Drovers and herdsmen whistled and cursed to control the rest of them and to bring them back to safe pasturage on Edom's side of the river. In the melee, others panicked and scrambled for the north bank, where they were quickly captured by Mesha's border guards.

Joram, Jehoshaphat, Edom's king, and their combined adjutants surveyed the situation from a nearby hill. Directly across from them, the sturdy fortress of Aineh menaced the fording place. Mesha's men could be seen clearly by all. They appeared to be well armed, well nourished, and eager for battle. Joram thought that his own troops, tired, thirsty and in disarray at the river, seemed a pitiful adversary.

With a curse, he turned to Jehoshaphat and made a sweeping gesture that encompassed the combined forces. "Has the Lord called the three of us together and brought us here to be defeated by Moab?"

His reference to the Lord was made out of a sense of politics rather than out of any genuine sense of belief in Jehovah.

Jehoshaphat knew it. Tall, rail-thin, and with the pallor of age, the Judean King continued to survey the situation as if Joram had not spoken. Edom's king, likewise, was silent.

Joram grew impatient. "Is it to be as I say, that we shall be defeated by Mesha?"

Slowly, Jehoshaphat turned, gave Joram a wan smile, and looked beyond him to the nearby circle of adjutants. "Is there not here a prophet of the Lord, that we may inquire of the Lord by him?"

Jehu spoke up in his deep, rumbling voice. "Yes, sire. There is a prophet of the Lord here."

Joram glanced around in surprise. "Who?"

"Elisha, sire."

"Elisha?"

"Yes, sire. He has been trailing us ever since we left our last encampment."

"Bring him to us at once," Joram snapped.

Jehu frowned, hesitated, then turned to obey the command.

But Jehoshaphat stopped him. "It is we who should seek him out. The word of the Lord is with Elisha. We do not order a prophet about as we would a slave."

And so it was that Joram, Jehoshaphat, and the King of Edom went down from the hill to search for Elisha, and to consult with him.

Joram saw him first and hailed him.

Elisha reined his horse to a stop.

"Your help, Elisha. We seek your help." Joram indicated the other two kings.

At the sight of Jehoshaphat, Elisha quickly dismounted, threw the reins to Gehazi, and salaamed. He also acknowledged the King of Edom with respect. But when he turned again to Joram, he bowed casually; and when he straightened, wariness etched his face.

For several seconds, the two men measured each other with open suspicion.

It was Joram who finally broke the stalemate. "Your help, Elisha. We need your help."

"You? Need *my* help? How can that be? You don't believe in my God. You should want no part of me. I certainly want no part of you. Go to the false prophets of your father and your mother."

"No," Joram countered instinctively, color flushing his face. Almost apologetically, he glanced at Jehoshaphat, and his voice took on a more careful tone. "We need to know if your god, 'the Lord,' as you call him, has led us here to be destroyed by the King of Moab."

Elisha made a scornful sound and looked at King Jehoshaphat as if he expected him to confess that Joram had coerced him into this alliance.

Instead, Jehoshaphat returned the look without wavering and said in a steady voice; "I have told Joram that my people and my horses are his to command. I have given him my word on that, Honored Prophet. I stand on it."

Grim resignation settled within Elisha. In a hard, low tone, he said to Joram, "I swear by the Lord God, I wouldn't bother with you if it weren't for the presence of King Jehoshaphat of Judah."

"I understand that. It is mutual." Joram ducked his head in a mock bow. "But what is your advice to us? How do we defeat Mesha with thirsty men and thirstier animals and a river almost bone dry?"

Elisha walked away a few paces to give himself space, remembering in detail the instructions which Elijah had given him for such a situation. They were not as easy to follow as he had assumed. He simply did not like Joram of Israel. He might as well admit it. Yet here he was as an intercessor with the Lord, and committed to helping Israel and Judah. He walked away a few more paces. Space and time. He needed both. Space away from the godless Joram and the vibrations he could feel being sent out from his unbelieving heart. And time to think. To meditate. To pray. To intercede. He couldn't talk to God, nor could he hear God speak to him, as long as anger burned so brightly in his own heart. Joram was an incendiary, an ember ready to burst into flame at any moment. How could he intercede for such an unbeliever?

"Well, what do you advise, Prophet?" Joram pressed.

Elisha faced him, and the others as well. "Bring me someone to play the lute for me. And give me a quiet place to reflect and to pray and to listen for the word of the Lord."

"You're no better than the priests of Baal," Joram scoffed, turning away. "They always want something given to them first, too. Although I must admit their price is higher than yours."

Jehoshaphat, on the other hand, ordered a tent prepared and a lute player provided. Then he led Joram and the King of Edom and all their adjutants back to their own encampment.

Elisha sequestered himself. The music of the lute soothed his mind and his spirit. He began to fast and to meditate and to praise the Lord in prayer. For a day and a night he fasted and prayed. In time, the message of the Lord came to him.

"The Lord says to fill this dry valley with trenches to hold the water he will send," he later reported to the kings and their adjutants assembled in Jehoshaphat's tent. "You won't see the wind or the rain, but this valley will be filled with water. You will have plenty for yourselves and for your animals."

Jehoshaphat accepted Elisha's words without hesitation. The King of Edom followed. But Joram's skepticism openly showed. Among the adjutants, only Jehu seemed to accept Elisha's report of the Lord's words as readily as Jehoshaphat. Though he said nothing, a look of undeniable fervor flickered in his eyes.

"But this is only the beginning," Elisha continued. "The Lord will make you victorious over the army of Moab. You will conquer the best of their cities, even those that are fortified. And you will ruin all the good land with stones." He turned and looked squarely at Joram. "It is a victory of and for the Lord God Jehovah."

Joram returned the look without comment, as if in his mind he already was attacking and could visualize his chariot leading the charge against Mesha's forces.

When it became evident that Joram would make no reply to Elisha's report, Jehoshaphat rose slowly to his feet. "Our gratitude, Honorable Prophet. Our gratitude to you. We praise the holy name of the Lord." He salaamed.

The King of Edom did likewise.

Reluctantly, Joram stood up. "Fill the valley with trenches, eh?"

Elisha nodded.

Joram addressed the King of Edom. "Since we are in your land, honored friend, would you want Edom's men to dig the trenches?"

"You defer to me with graciousness," the king replied. "Since it is the face of Edom that must be scarred by such digging, it is only right that my men should do it." He turned and started to instruct his adjutant to see that it was done.

Jehoshaphat stopped him. "If the Lord said for us to fill the valley with trenches, it will take more men than just the men of Edom to dig enough trenches. The Lord's gifts are bountiful. We can expect much water. The men from all three armies will share the duty."

Joram started to argue, but again Jehoshaphat prevailed. "Let us select half of each army to dig while the other half sees to our defenses, to the necessary guard duty, to the tending of the herds, and to the sundry other duties of encampment. We need to be as prepared to receive the Lord's gift of water as we must be prepared to receive his gift of victory over Moab."

The King of Edom glanced toward Joram questioningly. After all, they were there to help Israel.

"The Honorable Jehoshaphat is wise in the ways of The Lord," Joram concurred. "We will do as he says."

And so the order was given for half the men of Edom's army, and half the men of Judah's army, and half the men of Israel's army to dig great trenches all through the valley on the Edom side of the River Zered. They worked in shifts deep into the night, until the entire valley was pocked and slitted with trenches.

The next day, Jehoshaphat, Elisha, and other believers were at their prayers at earliest light. The priests traveling with Jehoshaphat had just offered the morning sacrifice when a great shout went up from the men of Edom at the far southeastern part of the encampment. The shout was picked up and relayed into the very heart of the camp, where the tents of all the kings were situated.

"Water!"

"Look!"

"Water!"

"It flows from the direction of Edom!"

"It's everywhere!"

"And our trenches are holding it!"

"They brim to overflowing!"

The sun had now reached the heights of Moab's mountains and reflected red and sullen on all the water in all the trenches in the entire valley, which lay on Edom's side of the Zered. The shouting and astonished jubilation of the armies of Israel, Judah and Edom increased.

The men of Moab rushed to see what caused all the commotion. When they saw the water red and sullen, they exclaimed, *"Blood!* The enemy kings are surely slain!"

"The enemy armies must have attacked and killed each other."

"Then let's go and collect the loot!"

But when the Moabites arrived at the Israelite camp, the combined armies of Israel, Judah and Edom rushed out and began killing them. The army of Moab fled. Behind them, the men of Israel moved forward into the land of Moab, destroying everything as they went. Day after day, they moved forward and spread destruction across the land. They destroyed walled cities. They threw stones on every good piece of land. They stopped up all the wells. They felled all the good trees.

Finally, only the fortress of Kir-haraseth was left standing. As a last resort, Mesha ordered seven hundred of his finest swordsmen to break through the invaders and kill the King of Edom. They failed. Kir-haraseth then took a deadly onslaught from Joram's forces.

To observe how their slingers were dealing the death blows to the fortress, Joram, Jehoshaphat, the King of Edom, and their adjutants stood in their chariots on a height of land. Elisha and Gehazi were on horseback a short distance away. They had accompanied the armies all the way, as witnesses to the devastating victory over Moab. And now Kir-haraseth was all but vanquished.

Yet no sign of surrender had yet been shown.

Jehu suddenly pointed off to the left, where one tall parapet of stone wall still remained. "There, sire! King Mesha has come to the wall."

Joram swiveled, leaned hard against the chariot's railing,

and stared in the direction Jehu pointed. "Who's that with Mesha?"

"His son. His eldest son. A lad of about twelve, I would say."

"What's Mesha doing?" Jehoshaphat asked, shading his eyes with one thin hand. "I see no sign of surrender. If not to surrender, why has he come to the wall?"

"He ought to admit defeat," Joram snapped impatiently.

"Agreed. But I see no sign."

Just then, a thin smudge of smoke curled up from the top of the wall. It lingered in the still, hot air uncertainly, then grew wider and made a telltale path of black against the coppery midday sky.

"Jehu," Joram ordered. "Send for the captain of the slingers. Find out what Mesha is up to."

"I'll go myself, sire. It will be quicker." He whipped his horses into a gallop and clattered forward. Dust boiled up from the chariot wheels.

A third and fourth figure appeared on the parapet next to Mesha and his son. But what they were doing was blotted out by the dust from Jehu's quick lunge forward. By the time the dust had settled and the parapet was once again in clear view, all activity appeared to have ceased. Only the wide, black path of smoke continued to laze upward. Then screams could be heard, agonized, sickening, unearthly.

Soon after, Jehu returned. He reined to a stop beside Joram's chariot. Even beneath the dust, his face was pale. His eyes were wide with disbelief.

"Well?" Joram demanded. "What is Mesha up to?"

Jehu swallowed hard. "He has . . . made us a . . . burnt offering, sire."

Smoke continued to issue from behind the wall.

"What kind of burnt offering?"

"His son, sire. His eldest son!"

-6-

Mesha's sacrifice of his eldest son stopped the battle.

Israel turned away in disgust.

So did the armies of Judah and Edom. Mesha neither officially surrendered, nor did he show any customary sign of accepting defeat.

Though destruction lay at every hand throughout Moab, the aggressors did not demand formal surrender. Those whose religious scruples allowed child sacrifice as an ultimate appeasement to Baal were offended by use of the act as a strategy of war. And those who were against all forms of human sacrifice, like Joram, were sickened by the action.

Joram motioned for his driver to turn the chariot away from the scene. Revulsion was visible in his dark face and glazed eyes. His lips were fixed in a stunned expression.

Elisha saw the reaction and found it surprising. He reined his horse and moved forward to ride alongside the royal chariot. "Mesha's act was not called for by the Lord," he shouted.

Joram cast a woeful and disbelieving look at him.

"That was an act of Baal worship. It was heathen and wrong."

Joram pulled off his helmet and ran a trembling hand through his hair.

"The Lord God Jehovah does not call for such human brutality to appease Him!" Elisha pulled the horse in closer to the chariot. "Such brutality is man's choice. It is an act of cowardice."

Joram glanced sharply at him.

"You do not have to believe me, Joram," he went on matter-of-factly. "Ask King Jehoshaphat. He'll tell you that what I'm saying is true."

"I didn't say it wasn't."

"Then you agree that Mesha's act was not called forth by Jehovah?"

Joram shook his head. "I don't know who called it forth. I only know that such an act is wrong."

Elisha shrugged. "It's common practice among those who worship Baal."

"Not in war."

"It is common practice," Elisha persisted. "For whatever reason."

"I don't believe in it." Joram spoke the words quietly, as if to himself.

Again, Elisha felt surprise.

"I don't believe in it," Joram repeated even more softly.

"Then put a stop to it," Elisha said.

Joram straightened and threw another sharp glance at him.

"You're the king," Elisha pressed. "Put a stop to child sacrifice in your kingdom."

Joram scoffed. "Stop child sacrifice? How could I put a stop to it?" He searched the face of the prophet and found only sincerity. Irritation nipped at him. What lunacy! Elisha was as impractical as Merari and as idealistic as Nahum. With an impatient curse, he ordered his driver to make faster speed toward the royal tents. "I have no interest and no time to argue with you, holy man. Not now. Not here."

Camp was broken without delay, farewells were made to the King of Edom and his army, and the order was given for the hosts of Israel and Judah to begin their return march. They took the shortest, most direct route through Moab to the Plain of Shittim and the fording place of The Jordan.

During this march, Joram successfully avoided Elisha. But when the host of Judah and the host of Israel crossed over The Jordan and were bivouacked near Jericho, a meeting with him could no longer be avoided. The two armies soon would go their separate ways. Jehu had reported that Elisha had every intention of returning to Samaria with the Army of Israel rather than going to Jerusalem with King Jehoshaphat. Joram knew he could expect to be the target of the holy man's stubborn efforts of persuasion. But in the meantime, he reminded himself, he owed a debt of gratitude to Jehoshaphat. Calling for Jehu to accompany him, he made his way to the tent of the King of Judah. To his displeasure, Elisha was already there.

"I have come to express my greatest gratitude to you, Honored King of Judah," Joram said, bowing low to Jehoshaphat. "You and your army brought much of our victory. I thank you."

"It is to the Lord God Jehovah you should be grateful, Joram. It is He who is responsible for our victory over Mesha." Jehoshaphat turned and motioned for Elisha to come forward.

Joram and Elisha once more confronted each other warily.

"Elisha told us true regarding the outcome of the battle with Moab," Jehoshaphat continued, "and he can be of great help to your kingdom. If you will let him, Elisha will tell you truth as he hears it from the Lord. You may not always like it, Joram. But Elisha will tell you true. That is a valuable thing to have as king, someone to tell you true."

Joram looked at Jehoshaphat, remembering how his father had always respected his counsel; and at the same time, wondering if Jehoshaphat's present urging of tolerance for Elisha's views was based on the wisdom of practical politics. Many complexities existed in the relationship between Israel and Judah. Not the least of those complexities was the constant, and common, search for ways to restrict the influence of Jezebel. Was this what Jehoshaphat was suggesting? Could Elisha be useful as a deterrent to Jezebel's influence?

Jehoshaphat patiently observed them both with detached

amusement. "You don't have to believe the same things. You don't even have to like each other. All you have to do is *use* each other to keep Israel and Judah safe from outside threats."

Elisha glanced at the old king in surprise and then began to laugh.

Joram felt surprise but no humor. He steeled himself against laughter. No need to let the holy man think he was won over. He wasn't. Until now, the only thing they had agreed on was their mutual hatred of child sacrifice. "In Moab, Elisha, you told me that I should put a stop to child sacrifice in the worship of Baal. I gave you no answer."

Elisha's laughter vanished.

Jehoshaphat narrowed his eyes and waited.

"Now, I give you my answer," Joram went on. "I give it now in gratitude to my friend, King Jehoshaphat of Judah. And in appreciation of his army's splendid performance on the field of battle."

"And what is your answer?"

"My answer is that I will destroy the pillar of Baal in the courtyard of the Ivory Palace in Samaria."

Elisha's eyes went wide.

In the far section of the royal tent, Commander Jehu looked up in astonishment.

A slow, approving smile spread across the gaunt face of King Jehoshaphat.

"Does this mean that you will also stop the practice of child sacrifice throughout—?"

"I did not say that!"

"But if you destroy the—"

"Let Joram finish," Jehoshaphat ordered quietly. "There is an altar near the pillar, which is also highly prized, I'm told. Let Joram tell us his plans for it, too."

"I have no plans for it," Joram answered in a flat tone. "Without the pillar, the altar is nothing."

"It's still a part of Baal worship. It, too, should be destroyed," Elisha insisted.

Resentment flared. "I'll destroy only the pillar. Nothing more!"

A momentary silence ensued.

Disappointment flickered in the old king's eyes, but he said, "Destruction of the pillar is a generous gift, Joram. I thank you for it. The host of Judah thanks you. As to your own people . . ."

"I can do no more. Not now. After all, I'm not even a believer in your Jehovah," Joram quickly defended.

Jehoshaphat sent a glance of caution toward Elisha.

Elisha made a formal salaam to them both and left the tent.

Early the next morning, Joram bid formal farewell to Jehoshaphat's army and led his own army northward toward Samaria. They bypassed Jezreel, where Jezebel and her entourage were in residence. And, to his pleasure, Elisha not only stayed away from him, he stayed completely out of sight for most of the journey. But thoughts of the previous evening's meeting with the prophet and the King of Judah were not put aside easily.

From the standpoint of practical politics, Joram realized that two separate issues had been involved in that meeting. One had to do with prohibiting child sacrifice; the other had to do with the prohibition of all Baal worship in the Northern Kingdom. That's what Elisha had pressured for. But to outlaw all Baal worship would be disastrous. It would cause a revolt throughout the land. There were not enough loyal men in the host of Israel to put down such a revolt. It was an impractical and a foolish idea.

And who could tell? Maybe the outright prohibition of child sacrifice would seem equally foolish to a population nurtured on the practice. Common sense told him, though, that such was not the case. Traditions of family closeness were strong, even among those who worshiped Baal. The prohibition of child sacrifice would be welcomed by the people; and the destruction of the pillar would let them know that he personally was against child sacrifice. They would also know that he was not under Jezebel's thumb.

He rode along at the head of his victorious army, reconsidering the importance of his decision to destroy the pillar, and thinking again of the fight with Moab. The excitement of war and the thrill of victory, even in retrospect, made the blood tingle in his veins. Such events of battle were a warrior's greatest treasure. At least for him they were. They were like rare jewels carefully wrapped in sheerest linen. The excitement and thrill of battle were to be carefully preserved in a gossamer of memory. At will, he could draw them forth from the timeless vault of his mind and re-live them once more.

Long ago, in his very first battle, he had learned to do this. Quite by accident, he had stumbled onto the fact that he could use such memories as an antidote to the horrors of pain and the stench of death. But the antidote failed him now. The final scene of battle with the Moabites at Kirharaseth, in which Mesha had made his ghastly sacrifice, swam before his eyes. He shook his head and, with a rough hand, wiped at his eyes to force the image back into the deepest recess of memory.

Maybe Elisha and Jehoshaphat were right, after all. Maybe he *should* destroy the altar as well as the pillar. Maybe he *should* go forward immediately to outlaw child sacrifice and all Baal worship. Why should anyone be willing to have children if the the dangers of ritualistic killings did not stop? Why indeed? he asked himself again. Maybe it was just such a fear that had kept Merari from having children. The thought popped into his mind from nowhere. Uncalled. Unexpected. Yet somehow fascinating. Of all the times he'd thought of Merari, wondered about her, dreamed and fantasized about her, that one particular thought never had come to him.

But it had now.

And the thought which followed made him ask himself if she would hate him less if he did, in fact, decree an absolute end to child sacrifice and Baal worship. But, then, on the other hand, why should it matter at all what she thought? Why should he still care about what she thought? In fact, Why should he care about what anybody thought? He was now king. He could do as he pleased.

He straightened up and shielded his eyes as the city gates of Samaria came into view in the hazy distance. He glanced over his shoulder. Elisha and his servant rode in silence several paces behind Jehu and the captains of the host.

"You need something, m'lord?" Jehu asked.

"The prophet. Tell him to come to the palace with us. I will wish to speak again with him."

Jehu looked puzzled, but he reined his horse immediately to do as his king had ordered.

Within an hour after their arrival at the Ivory Palace, Joram called Elisha, Jehu, and an astonished Obadiah to his private chambers to announce his decision that both the pillar and the altar of Baal in the palace courtyard were to be utterly destroyed.

"At first light on the morrow, it shall be done." He paused to drink deeply from a wine cup. The draught was cool and refreshing to his taste. He drank again, emptying the cup, feeling its deep, relaxing effect almost immediately. For the first time, he realized how tired he was. He reached for the flagon and refilled the wine cup. "Yes, first light on the morrow. That is the time they are to be destroyed. And all of us will be there. Along with anyone else you think should come. Except my mother, of course."

All three men waited in silence.

"In the meantime, Obadiah," he went on, "you are to have all the necessary edicts written and posted throughout the palace, and throughout the city. And, as usual, send couriers throughout the kingdom to post the notices everywhere." He saluted them with the wine cup. "Except Jezreel. Tell Jezreel last."

"Of course, sire," Obadiah agreed. "It shall be exactly

as you say. Jezreel and Queen Jezebel shall be told last of all."

"It's a good plan, sire," Jehu rumbled. "Even if the news may already be known to Queen Jezebel."

Joram glanced suspiciously at his aide. "Don't remind me of the spies we have in the palace. I know we have them. I also know it's your job to get rid of them. Is my trust misplaced? Or are you admitting failure?"

To cover Jehu's embarrassment, Elisha spoke up. "It matters little when Jezebel learns of this. What matters is that the destruction of Baal's pillar and altar will take place. And the act will be looked upon with great favor by Jehovah."

"Ah, yes." In mock solemnity, Joram refilled his wine cup, raised it, and drank again. "And now, I take my leave of you, sirs. I shall take this carafe of wine and find a bed."

"Shall I send you a woman, sire?" Obadiah's tone was matter-of-fact.

He shook his head.

All bowed as he turned and made his way toward an inner chamber.

Sleep came quickly to Joram, but in fitful restlessness. And only briefly, at that. In fact, much too briefly.

In the earliest hours of the morning, well before first light, Jezebel arrived from Jezreel and stormed into his private chambers accompanied by a tall eunuch. Joram's own manservant, Mano-ah, who had been dozing just inside the entry, tried to stop them, but he was no match for the muscular giant who shoved him roughly away.

Jezebel made straight for the couch where Joram lay sleeping and roughly shook him by the shoulder. "Abomination!"

He awakened with a dreadful start. Torchlight flickered so near that he felt its heat. Panic tore at him. He struggled upright, fearing fire, his head muddled with wine and exhaustion.

"Abomination!"

The repeated shout brought him fully awake.

Jezebel brandished a parchment in front of him. The eunuch with the torch moved closer, as if to protect his queen.

Joram shoved at the torch. "Get that away from me, fool!"

The eunuch stepped back. Near the entry, Mano-ah struggled to his feet and vanished into the darkness beyond the chambers.

"You will not destroy my altar!"

Joram snatched the parchment from her and swung off the couch.

"Who gave you such a right?" she demanded.

"And which of your spies brought you the news so quickly?" he parried with a hard laugh, shrugging into a robe.

"Who gave you the right to destroy the altar?" she repeated.

"I need no one's permission. I am now king."

"And by the gods condemned."

"But king, nevertheless."

She circled him like a she-leopard about to spring on her prey. "No, ingrate! You will not destroy my altar and my pillar."

"*Your* altar? *Your* pillar? I thought they belonged to Baal."

"*I* belong to Baal. And they are mine."

He scoffed.

"I will stop you."

He looked at her sharply. "How? With one eunuch and a torch?"

The corners of her mouth slipped into a strange smile. At that, a sliver of fear, unsummoned but familiar and haunting as a childhood memory, went through him.

She glanced toward the eunuch. "You think only two of us came from Jezreel?"

"I think it matters little how many there are of you," he brazened, turning and walking toward the entryway. "I have decreed that at first light the altar and pillar are to be destroyed. You cannot stop that."

"But I can stop you."

The eunuch, torch still in hand, moved swiftly to intercept him.

"You know the law," Jezebel menaced. "Unless you are there—physically present—the act of destruction cannot be committed."

Joram neither hesitated in surprise nor looked back. He simply shoved aside the great lion skin covering the entryway and ran. The corridor outside the sleeping chamber was pitch black. He ran instinctively until his vision adjusted itself and the shadowy hulk of walls and offshoot corridors began to emerge before him. What had happened to Mano-ah? Why had he not come back? And Obadiah? Where was Obadiah? And the palace guards? Where were they? Surely Jezebel had not laid siege to the entire palace!

He slowed his pace, realizing that she might have done just that. The places of Baal worship were that important to her. She would defend them at all costs. Even at the cost of imprisoning him—and more. Even at the cost of killing him!

Back down the corridor, he could hear the thudding steps of the pursuing eunuch. He stopped at an inset in the wall, pressed against it flat, and looked back. Grotesque fingers of smudgy torchlight crept toward him as the eunuch continued to pursue.

In a reflex action, he groped for the knife scabbard he normally wore. It was not there, of course. He kept no knife at the belt of his sleeping robe. He had no weapon. None. Except for the corded belt of his robe.

For a long moment, he remained pressed flat against the wall, considering whether or not he was tall enough and strong enough to throttle the eunuch fatally with the belt, or whether he should stay out of sight and get to the arms room for a sword and a knife. No man was better at the use of those weapons than he. His ultimate goal was personally to destroy the damnable pillar and altar. If he'd had any remaining doubts about the importance of that act, he certainly had none now. If Jezebel had taken all the others hostage she had not yet caught him. Nor would she. He was king. A king victorious over Moab. And now a king about to be victorious over Jezebel.

He slipped away from the wall, turned into a nearby offshoot corridor, and made his way to the arms room. The palace was still quiet. Apparently not a soul stirred. Did that mean Jezebel didn't have the place surrounded? he wondered, groping for a sword and a knife. At last his fingers closed over the hilts of each. Slipping out of the arms room, he went along another passageway to an inside stairway leading to the outer courtyard where the pillar and its altar were situated. At the top of the stairs, he hesitated and surveyed the empty courtyard. From what had already occurred, he had fully expected to see Jezebel's men encircling the altar and the pillar. But the courtyard appeared empty. Still, he hesitated. Warrior's instinct told him that danger lay at the foot of the stairs. Where was Mano-ah? And Obadiah? And, for that matter, the prophet Elisha?

Off to his right, where the passageway extended beyond the stairway, he heard the softest whisper. A tremor went through him. His hands tightened on the hilts of the sword and the knife. The whisper came once more. Carefully, he turned, trying to see into the deepest shadows of the passageway. For the third time, the whisper came, this time loudly enough for him to understand it. "Sire, it is I, Jehu."

"Come forward."

Jehu emerged.

In spite of himself, Joram breathed a sigh of relief.

"I see that Mano-ah got back to you with the palace guards. I'm glad. I would have come myself, except for the need to defend against the—"

"Wait! What do you mean? Mano-ah and the guards never came to my chambers. I had to flee my chambers. Alone. With the Queen's eunuch chasing me."

Astonishment filled Jehu's face.

"The Queen Jezebel wishes to keep me from this place. She was prepared to harm me. Where were the guards? And for that matter, where were you?" Though his words were whispered, the accusation was strong.

"Here, sire. And the majority of the palace guards are here." Jehu pointed toward the perimeter of the courtyard. "All around the courtyard in the shadows. We are waiting to defend against Queen Jezebel's forces. We understand they are inside the palace."

A vein pounded in his neck. "You realize what you're saying?"

Jehu said nothing.

"Well, do you? My mother virtually laid siege to this place while we all slept!"

Jehu stiffened, offended.

"Never mind," Joram said in a tone of clear disgust. He turned and pointed toward the shadows in the passageway. "Is there anyone else back there?"

"Yes, sire. Elisha, the prophet."

"Then bring him along. Let's do the deed now and rid the palace of Jezebel." He turned and hurried down the stairway, trailed by Jehu and Elisha.

At the bottom of the stairway, Jehu called for the captain of the palace guards to have a small battering ram carried forward. It was done; and as Joram struck the first blow to the top of the stone pillar, six soldiers hefted the battering ram and slammed it into the side of the pillar near its base. The battering ram again found its target, and the pillar toppled. Pieces and chunks of stones spilled onto the ivory and mosaic floor, scattering everywhere.

The sound of stone shattering and giving way carried to all parts of the palace. People could be seen scurrying toward the courtyard from every direction.

"Light the torches," Jehu commanded the guards.

This, too, was done; and the orange flames flared and flickered brightly over the scene to reveal a cordon of palace guards around the entire area. If Jezebel's forces were in the palace, they would have to fight hard to stop him now.

"The horses," he ordered. "Bring the horses with the pull-ropes!" He moved close to the altar and slashed at the wooden superstructure carved in the image of Baal. Then, with the tip of his sword, he pricked the cobalt stones out of the face of the idol. When he once again slashed at the figure, it splintered. Meanwhile, the pull-ropes had been put in place. The horses pulled, toppling the stone footings and side walls of the altar.

In short order, the destruction of the pillar and the altar of Baal had been accomplished. Jagged remains of wood and stone littered the courtyard. Those who had observed the destruction were absolutely silent. No human sound could be heard, until Jezebel scurried onto the scene, face stricken and pale, eyes filled with horror and fear. For a long moment she stared at the destruction, then turned to Joram as if to curse him.

Before she could speak, Elisha stepped up to stand beside Joram. "Thou shalt not make unto thee any graven image. Thou shalt have no other gods before me, saith the Lord God Jehovah."

Rage overrode the fear in her eyes. Her lips parted, but no sound emerged. Defeated, she crumpled at the feet of the prophet of God.

-7-

The news of Joram's destruction of the royal altar spread throughout the kingdom like dust before strong wind. Its particles filtered into every crevice of every soul. While reactions varied according to background and beliefs, it impacted lives, influenced business transactions, and affected relationships. Some citizens were repulsed by what Joram had done. Some were skeptical. Some found it amusing. Some were angry over it. But the majority welcomed it. And nowhere in the kingdom was the news more welcome than in the house of Nahum and Merari.

Notices dispatched from Joram's palace had arrived in Shunem on the very morning the destruction took place. They had been tacked up on the city gates, and the elders of Shunem read them to the people, discussed them, and spread the word to surrounding homes and villages. But it was Elisha's version that most interested Nahum and Merari when he came through a few days later on his way back to Carmel.

They were in the courtyard, where a cooling breeze riffled the late day's heat and refreshed the shadows cast by the surrounding house.

Nahum grinned as Elisha finished describing Jezebel's attempt to hold Joram hostage in his own bedchambers.

Elisha reached for a piece of fruit from the tray in front of him. "You know how suspicious I've been of him."

"And rightly so," Nahum said.

"But he did do something good." Merari's voice was so quiet she might have been speaking to herself. "Moving against child sacrifice is a very good thing. Can you imagine what it would be like to have your child snatched from you and killed in the name of religion?" She looked over at the prophet, her face pale and full of sorrow.

Nahum pinned her with a quizzical gaze. "Whatever Joram's actions, they were done for himself, beloved."

"Of course," she said. "He has respect for no gods and for only a few people."

Nahum went to her and put his hands on her shoulders.

"Well, even so, a major change in the affairs of the souls of men has occurred in this kingdom," Elisha said. "I believe that change will affect other kingdoms, as well, because of Joram's actions."

"You're probably right, Prophet," Nahum conceded good-humoredly. "But I'm a man of the soil, not of motivations or intrigues or politics." His tone indicated clearly that he was ending the conversation. He looked down at Merari. "Are you ready?"

Her sorrowful and serious expression lifted. She nodded and stood up.

In surprise, Elisha, too, stood up.

Merari smiled at him. "We mean no rudeness, Elisha. But we have something we want you to see."

Elisha glanced questioningly from one to the other.

"It is nothing to fear," Nahum reassured him, turning and leading the way out of the courtyard, through the house, and out toward the main gate of the compound.

Libn walls, ten to twelve feet high, extended east and west of the main entry gate to form the south wall of the compound. At the gate itself, the walls were only about two feet thick. But as they extended away from the gate on either side to intersect with the compound's east and west walls, their thickness widened inwardly to about twelve feet. At its widest, the top of the wall created a good-sized flooring for a second-story room. And, in fact, such a room had been built at the southwest corner. A narrow, open stairway on the inside face of the wall led up to this new room. Nahum and Merari led Elisha up the stairway and into the room. Gehazi and Tamar were standing just inside, grinning broadly, their eyes on Elisha.

His face wrinkled into a puzzled frown. Nahum gestured for him to look around. The room was furnished with a bed, a stool, and a table, on which rested a bowl of fruit, cheeses, a pitcher of goat's milk, and a lamp.

Elisha made a slow, full turn, trying to comprehend.

"It's yours, Elisha," Merari said. "We hope it will be a comfortable retreat for you."

"Come and go as you like," Nahum added.

Elisha made another full turn. In a far corner, almost hidden from view, was a reed mat with a goatskin coverlet for Gehazi. Windows were cut in the south and north walls to catch every errant breeze.

"It's for you, master!" Gehazi blurted out, unable to keep silent any longer.

Elisha shook his head, still in the grip of astonishment.

"Oh, but it *is,* master." Gehazi reassured him. "And it's for me, too!"

His joy was infectious. Merari giggled in spite of herself.

Elisha looked to Merari and then to Nahum again as if seeking reassurance of the gift's reality. "No one has ever given such a present to a poor man of God."

Nahum gave a great laugh and clasped Elisha's shoulder. "The room is yours. It will be quieter here for you than at the house of the elder priest in the village."

"And to think, master," Gehazi piped, "it will be such a rest for your weary servant, too. No more trudging about, searching for and begging borrowed mats and coverlets. It's all here for us both!" He made an expansive gesture which included the blushing Tamar.

Laughter erupted!

Gehazi looked surprised. Then, realizing what he had implied, he blushed even more fully than Tamar.

In spite of reservations about Gehazi, Merari found herself thinking that maybe Tamar was right about him. Maybe he could be honorable and true. Maybe his loyalty to Elisha was the key to his character. Maybe Tamar wouldn't be hurt by him, after all.

As their laughter faded, Elisha grew serious, looked at Merari and Nahum. "How can I ever repay you?"

"No repayment is expected," Nahum assured him. "We simply want to be of help to you, Elisha."

"It is our way of showing that we, too, believe in the Lord God Jehovah," Merari added.

Elisha held out his hands to each of them. "Then let me share with you a prayer. A prayer of thanksgiving."

Gehazi immediately moved closer to Elisha, knelt, and took hold of the hem of his robe. With his left hand, he motioned for Tamar to come and kneel beside him. She did so at once. He clasped her hand and both bowed their heads.

There was something innocent and wonderful in the action. Again Merari wondered if she had misjudged Gehazi. She hoped so, since Tamar appeared to be truly in love with him.

Elisha looked heavenward and began to pray: "Great God Jehovah, the one true God, we praise your holy name."

Merari moved closer to Nahum and bowed her head.

"In thanksgiving, O God, we come to you to express our joy in the friendships you have given us. We sing your praises and seek your blessings on this household. Let love abide in this place for all of us who rest here. Let the peace of kinship lighten our days and soften the darkness of our nights. Amen."

As he finished the prayer, Elisha bowed his head. Still holding tightly to their hands, he let silence engulf them.

The poignancy of the moment and the simplicity of Elisha's words touched Merari. Tears filled her eyes, and she squeezed Nahum's hand.

He responded in kind and whispered, "All is well."

But later that night, deep in the stillness of their own room after they had made love, Nahum asked, "Do you ever regret having married me?"

His tone was so casual that for a moment she thought he was teasing. "Of course. I regret it at least thirty times a day!"

"I am serious, Merari. Do you ever regret having married me?"

She raised up on one elbow and peered at him through the pale light provided by a small nearby lamp. "What a question! What on earth—?"

"Do you?"

"Why would you even think such a thing?"

"I am not sure. Maybe I thought of it when you defended Joram today."

His words stunned her.

"When Elisha was telling us the details about the destruction of Baal's altar and pillar, you defended Joram. Maybe *approved* is a better word. It made me wonder, that's all."

She tried to recall the afternoon's conversation.

"You said he did something good," Nahum reminded her. "It is the first time in all the years of our marriage I have heard you say something in approval of him. But more than that, I think it was the look on your face when you spoke of the children who would be spared from cruel sacrifice."

Fresh astonishment went through her. In a very careful tone, she said, "It was Joram's actions I approved of. I thought you did, too. Thousands of people will now feel safer about their children."

"Of course, but that's not the point."

"What is the point, my husband?"

"Children, Merari. Children."

"What about them?"

"Perhaps you would have a child, beloved, if you had married—"

She stopped him by pressing a finger to his lips. "Don't say it. Don't even think it! I love *you*, Nahum. I always have." Heart sinking, she lay back on the bed and frowned up into the darkness. Why had God withheld a child from them? Why? And now, after all these years of childless marriage, why should the pain of that fact re-emerge so acutely? Would neither of them ever accept their childlessness?

Nahum turned to her, moved closer, and encircled her with his arms. "Forgive me. It was just that I saw such pain and sadness in your face this afternoon. Forgive me."

In the days and weeks which followed, neither of them spoke of the incident, but it was never far from Merari's mind. She made a special effort to show Nahum her love, in spite of all the busyness of harvest activities; and she began saying additional prayers of praise and thanksgiving for him. "Dear Lord God, I praise your holy name for giving me a man strong in will and sweet in nature, faithful in his love for me, as I must continue to be for him. Protect him, O Lord, from all evil." Even in the busiest of days, she made time to say prayers for him and for their marriage. Nahum's work never ceased. Her own days were filled with managing the household, preparing and sending food to the poorer families in the area. Her mother and father returned from their visit in Joppa, adding to the household responsibilities.

And Elisha and Gehazi came and went frequently from the room on the wall. The more frequently they came, and the longer they stayed, the greater became the sense of peace pervading the house in Shunem. Her father and Nahum claimed it was because they owned no slaves. "The stench of that misery and sadness has never been allowed to settle here."

But there was another reason. There had to be. Ever since they had given the room to Elisha, Merari had been aware of a special aura of peace that was an entirely new experience. There seemed to be a new dimension of spiritual awareness, as if an angel of the Lord had taken up residence, too.

Then came the time for Elisha to go away for an extended period of time. He turned to Gehazi, busy with the packing of their few goods, and said, "I would like to do something for Merari and Nahum. This room is such a marvelous gift. What can I give them in return? What gift could even begin to match their generosity?"

Elisha had said it in such a way that Gehazi knew it was not a question requiring an answer. Besides, he had his mind on quite another matter. Tamar was irritated with him, though he didn't know exactly why. He went on with the packing.

"Gehazi?"

"Sir?"

"Call this Shunammite woman. Call Merari. Have her come here, please."

With a sigh, Gehazi complied.

Within a very few minutes, Merari was standing in the doorway.

Elisha smiled at her, and motioned for her to come in.

She moved easily toward him. "How can I help you, my friend?"

"It is you I would like to help," he returned. "You and Nahum."

"Help?" she asked, puzzled.

"Your generosity is so great. Isn't there something I can do for you in return?"

She smiled at him, but shook her head.

He glanced at the servant. "Gehazi, *you* say now to her, 'Look, you have been concerned for us with all this care. What can I do for you?' "

Gehazi's eyes went wide. "Me, sir?"

Elisha nodded.

"But, but, if she . . ." His eyes went wider. "How can *I* ask? If she will say nothing for you, m'lord, why should she say something for me?"

Merari laughed gently. "We have our thanks, Elisha. You are our friend. Anyway, this room seems such a small gift for so great a man of God!"

Elisha silently concentrated on tracing one finger along an imaginary line of the table top. "Perhaps," he said finally, "perhaps I could speak to the king on your behalf?"

A small wave of surprise went through her. It was a strange comment, since Elisha knew of the close court connections she and Nahum already had through her father and Uncle Obadiah. She studied him for a moment, wondering if he knew that Joram had not yet reappointed Nahum as Royal Overseer. Then she decided that even if he did know, he was not the man to speak in Nahum's behalf in that matter. "I dwell among my own people," she softly replied.

With an understanding nod, he sighed. "Then all I can do is thank you again."

"I bid you a good journey, Elisha." She turned and left.

He followed after her as far as the door and watched as she made her way back down the stairs, across the open area of the compound, and into the main house. "She's a great woman, Gehazi. I wish I could do something for her and for Nahum. There must be *something* they would like to have." His tone was almost wistful.

"Well, m'lord, they seem to have everything." Gehazi stuffed a parchment scroll into the goatskin duffel. "Except a son, of course."

Elisha turned sharply and stared at the servant.

"Not that you can do anything about that."

Slowly, Elisha moved back across the room to the south window and stared out as if hearing some distant sound.

"I suppose that Nahum, fine a man as he is, is just too old now to give her a son. At least that's what Tamar seems to think." Gehazi picked up Elisha's extra pair of sandals and crammed them into the duffel alongside the parchment. "Tamar tells me they've been married for a very long time. They're devoted to each other. She says her mistress has confided that they have tried often to have a child. But it just hasn't happened for some reason." He glanced around, looking for other items to be packed, and for the first time realized how long his master had been staring out the window. He let go of the duffel and peered at him. "M'lord?"

Elisha neither moved nor broke his meditative silence.

Gehazi backed away, recognizing the familiar trancelike state that had come over his master. It happened often. It was a strange, inexplicable state. It happened to his master just as it had happened to the great prophet Elijah. And always, when it occurred, the results were visionary. For at such times, Elisha could hear the voice of the Great God Jehovah. Gehazi backed further away and stood quietly. Outside, sounds from the courtyard drifted up and faded against the silence that deepened and lengthened in the room. His mind turned to Tamar, and he began to feel an unhappy impatience. He changed position and shuffled his feet. As he did, Elisha moved.

"Gehazi?"

"Sir?"

"Call the Shunammite," Elisha said in a faraway voice.

"Sir, she was just here."

"Call Merari, I say! Call her here again."

"Yes, m'lord. At once." He turned and scampered down the stairway to do his master's bidding.

When Merari, followed by the servant, entered the room, Elisha still stood by the window, staring out. She waited, expecting him to acknowledge her arrival; but he didn't move. She waited a few seconds longer, then asked, "Did you want to see me, Elisha?"

He turned. When she saw the strangely brooding look in his eyes, she tensed. "You have need of something, Elisha?"

Behind her, she heard Gehazi impatiently shuffling with the half-packed duffel.

"Is all well with you, Elisha?"

His brooding look lifted. He came toward her, and in the

most gentle of tones said, "Merari. About this season next year, according to the time of life, you shall embrace a son."

She heard his words, understood their meaning even through the layers of astonishment. But she did not believe them. Not for a moment. What a cruel joke! And from a man like Elisha.

"Did you hear what I said, Merari?"

She continued to stare at him.

"You believe me, don't you?"

"No, m'lord, I do not believe you." Unwanted tears filled her eyes. "Man of God, do not lie to your maidservant."

A stricken look filled Elisha's face.

Merari turned and ran from the room.

-8-

But Merari did conceive. She bore Nahum's son as Elisha had prophesied.

"He's beautiful," she murmured.

"Handsome," Nahum corrected in a whisper. With the tip of his index finger, he stroked one of the baby's tiny fists. The baby stirred and grasped his finger. "He is strong, too."

"He is Ozem. 'In God's Power.' "

"We have named him well," Nahum grinned.

A small frown began to crease the space between Merari's eyes. "When I think back to what awful thoughts I held for Elisha the day he prophesied we would have a son, I'm ashamed.

Nahum laughed softly.

"Really," Merari protested, as if for the first time. "When he first prophesied we would have a child . . . well . . . I thought . . ." She gave a shake of her head. "What awful thoughts I did have!"

Nahum chuckled. "Elisha understood. He is often disbelieved when he speaks of the things that God has planned."

"Then you believed him from the very first?"

Nahum looked rather sheepish. "Does it matter now?" He put his arm about her shoulders, pulled her and the baby closer to him, and held them until the sounds from the other part of the house indicated that more guests were arriving to rejoice with the household over the birth of Ozem.

The child had been circumcised on the eighth day of his

life, in the Hebrew tradition. Elisha had attended him, along with the elder priest of Shunem. And now a great feast had been prepared. The entire village had been invited. So had many friends from Samaria and other cities in the Northern Kingdom who were friends of Benaiah and Zibia and Uncle Obadiah. Still others, who had been invited but were unable to make the trip, had sent gifts.

Athaliah had been especially thoughtful. She had sent a silver cup, plate, and spoon graven with Ozem's initials, and with the royal crest of Judah as the hallmark on each piece. For Merari, she had sent a beautiful shawl woven of the sheerest linen and embroidered with the symbol of a long and happy life, the pomegranate. For Nahum, she had sent a marvelous tunic embroidered with the same symbol, and a magnificently rich silver-studded belt.

It was a time of great rejoicing. Merari and Nahum had a son! In the courtyard, extra tables had been set up to hold the foodstuffs. Guests mingled around them, sampling from great loaves of brown breads, barley cakes, and oaten biscuits; figs, dates, grapes, and apples; steaming bowls of lentils and greens; steaming sides of beef and racks of lamb and venison and hare. The prophets' school at Jericho had sent great baskets of oranges as Elisha's gift to this wondrous feast. In this part of the Northern Kingdom, if any lived in hunger they were either lazy in their work, uncaring in spirit, or not included at this feast of rejoicing for the son of Nahum and Merari.

Music was everywhere. Lute and lyre, timbrel and brass, reed and tambourine. Uncle Obadiah had seen to that by arranging for the presence of the court musicians from the Ivory Palace in Samaria.

But beyond all the display of plenty, over and above the pleasures of friends and camaraderie, was the marvelous knowledge that Nahum and Merari finally had produced a son. After twelve years of childlessness, an heir to the family name, traditions, and lands was a reality. Alive! A son alive!

Healthy and bright through the power of God's own good grace. And Elisha, the man of God, had prophesied his birth.

Throughout the kingdom, his prophecy was spoken of in tones of awe and deepening respect—both for him personally and as the representative of the Great God Jehovah.

"This is a great occasion," said the elder priest of Shunem to Nahum as he came into the courtyard escorting Merari and the baby so carefully cradled in her arms. Merari's old nurse, Achsa, hovered at her heels, almost as though doubting Merari's ability to hold the child.

Elisha smiled and bowed in greeting to the elder priest.

"It is a great occasion," the priest repeated in his customary fashion. "A great occasion."

"My heart is filled to overflowing," Nahum agreed, watching Merari move past him to show off the baby to a group of women on the far side of the courtyard.

"It is a great and joyous occasion," the priest from Shunem repeated for the third time.

Nahum turned to Elisha. "Everyone approves of my son, it seems."

"And so they should. He's a gift from God. And just as his name says, the child is in His gracious power."

"Uncle Obadiah says he will grow to be a strong man."

"I expect your uncle is right. The boy will grow strong in many ways," Elisha returned.

"And why not?" the elder priest from Shunem interjected. "Why not indeed? With a friend like you, Honorable Prophet, and with a father like Nahum, why shouldn't the boy grow strong?"

Before either Nahum or Elisha could utter a word, the old priest hurried on, obviously enjoying his chance to lay flattery upon compliment before two eminent listeners. "Now you take Nahum, here. He's the most hard-working man you could hope to find. And what's more, he's the finest overseer the king could have. There may be lots of things we don't like about King Joram, but he did a good thing in reappointing Nahum as his Royal Overseer here in the Plain of Jezreel. . . ."

The rest of the priest's words went unheard. The elation Nahum had been feeling dulled. The truth of the matter was, of course, Joram had *not* reappointed him Royal Overseer. And now that he had a son, the reappointment was more important than ever. It had been two years since Joram had become King of Israel; and still he had sent no official proclamation of reappointment. Neither, of course, had he done anything to indicate that he wanted Nahum out. Joram simply had ignored the whole matter.

Now, as Nahum thought about it, that was the most demoralizing thing of all. Was his post so unimportant that it warranted no action? Was he of such low rank in the hierarchy of the royal court that his position was taken for granted? Or was it because of the far more personal enmity between them?

These questions were not new ones. He had asked them of himself many times in the past two years. More than once, he had determined to go to Joram and confront him about the situation. But in each instance, Benaiah and Uncle Obadiah had advised against such a confrontation. He felt foolish over having let the situation continue in silence. Now that there was a son to think of, an heir to a tradition of status and worth and responsibility for the land, perhaps he should confront Joram.

Elisha nudged him, drawing him back to the moment and at the same time interrupting the talkative priest. "Your other friends are waiting to see you, too, Nahum."

The elder priest looked momentarily startled, then apologized for detaining Nahum and moved away.

"From the look on your face, my friend," said Elisha, "your thoughts must have carried you far away. What subdued your spirit so quickly?"

"It is of small account," Nahum parried, walking on

through the courtyard to greet other guests with a nod or a wave.

But Elisha would not be put off. He followed alongside. Because he did, none of the other guests came near, assuming that they had no right to intrude on a visit between host and holy man. Finally, when they reached the far side of the courtyard where the fewest number of guests were, and where they could not be overheard, Nahum relented and told Elisha of his concern about his reappointment as Royal Overseer.

A hard look came into Elisha's eyes.

"I know that Joram has many things on his mind. Things that are much more critical than a farmer's reappointment," Nahum went on. "There was the war with Moab, the constant border skirmishes with Ben-Hadad's Damascus raiders, the faltering relations with Tyre and Sidon because of Jezebel."

"Jezebel!" Elisha spat out the name in disgust. "She's publicly denouncing your son."

"Yes, I know," Nahum said flatly.

Elisha's face colored. "She does more than that. She defiles your wife with lies! Jezebel is saying that I'm the father of your child. Did you know that?"

Nahum gave a curt nod.

For a long moment, the two friends measured each other with mutual candor and respect.

"Does Merari know of this awful lie?"

Nahum shook his head. "I hope she never does. It would serve no good purpose. None at all."

"Jezebel's evil is against God."

"But human beings are her victims."

"Including her own son. She prays and plots for vengeance against Joram because he destroyed the pillar and the altar."

"What an evil!"

"Someday the old prophecy of God's curse on her will be fulfilled."

The two men stood silent for several seconds, looking out across the courtyard and reconsidering the realities of evil and how vulnerable they were to them.

Everyone was a victim, Nahum decided. Joram included. "Maybe it is just an oversight, after all," he said, half to himself.

"What's an oversight?"

"My reappointment."

The hard look came again into Elisha's eyes. "It's no oversight. Joram deliberately ignores you. It's his way."

From the far side of the courtyard, a stir and commotion distracted them. They saw Benaiah and Obadiah walking purposefully toward the main salon of the house. At the same time, Kallai came hurrying toward them.

"What's all the commotion?"

"We have an unexpected guest."

"Who?"

"The king!"

"Speak of the devil, eh, Elisha?" he said in astonishment. He turned, looking for Merari; but she was hidden from view by the cluster of women still chattering and admiring the baby.

"Tell Merari of the king's arrival, Kallai. I shall see to his greeting." He turned toward the house, closely followed by Elisha.

Nahum was unprepared for what he found in the main salon. Joram stood near the center of the room, accepting greetings from Benaiah and Obadiah. At his side was a crowd of slaves with boxes, bales, crates, casks, and assorted packages. There were at least two dozen slaves, both men and women. Each wore a distinctive cumberbund bearing Joram's crest.

Commander Jehu stood to one side. He, too, wore a cumberbund embroidered with Joram's crest. But his was half-hidden by the wide belt from which hung the scabbard and short dagger he was never without. As Nahum and

Elisha came across the room, Jehu salaamed with great courtesy.

Joram, as if not to be outdone, breached royal protocol by hailing them.

"Be alert, my friend," Elisha warned. "He wants something."

"Your wife, Nahum," Joram greeted. "Where is Merari?"

"She is with our guests in the courtyard."

"Guests? Am I intruding on a gathering of guests?" The mocking tone was insulting.

Nahum planted himself squarely in Joram's way. Elisha closed rank beside him.

"I want to see her. And your new son. As you can see, I've brought gifts. For them both."

"Your visit gives this house much honor, sire." Benaiah bowed.

"But you have taken us by surprise," Obadiah added, casting a look of caution toward Nahum. "That accounts for our seeming lack of hospitality. We must apologize."

"No matter," Joram answered, surprisingly agreeable. "It would not be my wish to intrude on your guests. Bring Merari and the baby to me in some quiet part of the house." He turned to Nahum. "In the meantime, I need a word with you, my host."

Nahum tensed.

Benaiah, Obadiah, and Elisha did not move.

"In private," Joram added, walking to a far corner of the big room.

"Go, my nephew," Obadiah urged. "It's the word about your reappointment. I told you he would get around to it."

"I shall fetch Merari and the baby at the proper time," Benaiah offered, turning away and taking Obadiah and Elisha along with him.

"Be alert, my friend," Elisha repeated over his shoulder.

Nahum gave a slight nod, looked again at the crowd of

slaves waiting in the center of the room, and went to Joram. "If your people are hungry, there is plenty in the cooking area for them."

"Always the perfect host, eh, Nahum?"

"It's the custom of this household to offer food to all who come here."

"My people are well fed. They have no need of your food."

"Very well. What is it you want to talk to me about, then?"

"Your reappointment as Royal Overseer. Do you want it?"

A tremor went through Nahum's gut.

"If it pleases you to make the reappointment."

"It doesn't. And you damn well know it."

"Then why discuss it?" His boldness surprised him.

"Because it will no doubt please Merari. Especially now, since the birth of the son Elisha gave you."

Anger shot through Nahum. He tensed, holding himself back to keep from hitting Joram's sneering face.

"Forgive me. I should have said prophesied, shouldn't I?" Joram quickly added, turning away and changing the subject. "My inspectors tell me that seven of your fields have not yet been planted this season. Is that true?"

"It is," Nahum said, still feeling the heat of anger.

"Why haven't they been planted?"

"It is the fallow year for those fields."

"That's a Hebrew custom."

"It is a good farming custom."

"Superstition!"

"Practical land management," Nahum insisted.

"The practice is outlawed in my kingdom. It reduces yield."

Nahum stepped toward him. "Worn-out land won't produce enough to feed your kingdom. Have a caution how you abuse the land, sire."

"Fallow land is outlawed in this kingdom," Joram repeated. "If you want your reappointment, you must use all your fields every season. *All* of them!" He reached inside his tunic, pulled out an official document, and thrust it toward him.

Nahum took it.

Joram brushed past him, motioned for Jehu to follow, and went in search of Benaiah, Merari, and the new baby.

Elisha reappeared from another part of the house and questioned Nahum with a look.

He handed Elisha the document. "My appointment. It's conditional."

"On the yield of the land?"

"In effect," Nahum shrugged. "He wants me to ignore the practice of the fallow year."

"Ah." A deeper understanding showed in Elisha's eyes.

"It is a good and practical use of the land to let it rest every seventh year." Nahum spoke almost as if to himself.

"It's also God's command that men do so," Elisha reminded him.

"I didn't tell Joram that."

"It's the most important reason why you practice the custom of the fallow year. Did you tell him *that?*"

A smile spread slowly over Nahum's face. "Do you suppose he would have understood the idea of a power higher than himself?"

-9-

First light, gray and soft and silent as the land, pushed at the canopy of night. Normally, such a dawn was cool, unfettered by heat. *This* dawn, however, showed no such mercy. It brought no surcease from the heat of yet another harvest season.

Merari stepped from the house, dabbed at her forehead with a square of cotton cloth, and looked up at Mount Moreh's smudged imprint in the widening gap of dawn.

Even it had a certain wilted look, she decided, wishing she had taken Ozem and gone with Zibia for a visit in Philistia. It would be lovely on the seacoast this time of year, with dawns as crisply cool as this one was sere and hot here in the Plain of Jezreel.

But because it was harvest season again, and because there was so much to be done, she hadn't seriously entertained the idea of going. Nahum had urged her to go, but she couldn't bring herself to leave him. Not at harvest time.

It had been almost seven years since he had received his conditional reappointment as Royal Overseer from Joram. They both had worked hard to see that it remained in effect. So successful were their efforts that even if Joram had thought of withdrawing the reappointment, he would have found himself blocked by the very condition he'd placed on it. Not once had the annual yields diminished. Even though Nahum continued to practice the Hebrew custom of the fallow year, and rotated his fields and the grains which grew in them.

Nahum gave all the credit for such abundance to the Lord God Jehovah. For every field tilled, for every vineyard tended, for every seed planted, he openly confessed and practiced his belief in the Lord's hundredfold principle as proclaimed to the Hebrew patriarchs.

Benaiah and Uncle Obadiah claimed that Joram never mentioned Nahum, though he often inquired about Merari and about the boy, Ozem.

Ozem! She smiled to herself. He was already seven years old. Nahum had promised that this year he could go to the fields to help with the harvest. How quickly he had grown. Sometimes she still found it hard to realize that finally, after so many years of barrenness, the Lord had given them that most precious of all gifts, a son. A deep, satisfied feeling went through her. He was such a bright and healthy child, with a sweet, endearing temperament.

"When I grow up," he had told his nurse, Achsa, and Kallai on a recent day, "I want to be a farmer just like my father."

"But what about your grandfather? I thought you wanted to be like him."

The boy thought for a moment.

"He travels a lot," Achsa prompted. "You like to travel."

"Like Elisha?"

"No, child. Not like Elisha. Elisha is a holy man of God. Your grandfather is an important man in King Joram's royal court."

"Is my father important, too?"

The old nurse put down her mending and gathered the boy to her. "He is the most important man you will ever know, Ozem. And one of the kindest."

"Then I want to be like him, Achsa. *Just* like him."

Merari smiled again, thinking of her son and of the added dimension of love he had brought into the household. "All is well," she murmured.

A night bird called; and from afar, she heard the bleating of sheep as a shepherd moved a flock to a higher, cooler pasture. Soon the rest of the household would rouse. The work of another harvest-season day would begin, with a great many details to be supervised.

She resisted the intrusion of such practical thoughts, wanting, rather, to make the good memories last, wanting to luxuriate in the quiet of aloneness for just a few more moments. But the gentle quality of her reverie had been replaced by memories of much harder things. She walked slowly around the open space between the main house and the pottery shed, thinking how harsh the world around them seemed. Skirmishes with Syria on Israel's borders grew more and more frequent. Ben-Hadad of Damascus, ambitious for added territory, pressed Joram to become his ally in a war against Syria. But Joram was hesitant, not quite trusting Ben-Hadad. Benaiah speculated that the most recent increase in border skirmishes was another of Ben-Hadad's attempts to force Joram into an alliance. He traveled often now to Damascus, and to Tyre and Sidon as well, in an effort to keep open the important trade routes and to maintain existing treaties.

Elisha had even offered to go to Ben-Hadad and to the King of Syria, to warn them of God's power in behalf of Israel if they pressed for war. But before he could make full plans for such a trip, religious unrest within Israel rose to alarming proportions pushed by an unrelenting Jezebel and her Baal priests.

When King Jehoshaphat of Judah died, Jezebel seized that opportunity to agitate openly against Jehovah in Judah. "Now that my weak and sickly son-in-law is the new King of Judah, the worship of Baal can be impressed on all citizens" she was reported to have boasted.

Boldly, she sent her couriers and her Baal priests out into all the lands of both Israel and Judah with instructions to tell the people that the worship of Baal was more powerful than ever, and that child sacrifice was no longer royally condemned. It was a lie, but the news caused riots and fighting to disrupt otherwise peaceful villages and cities. New altars to Baal were built everywhere.

To restore the peace, Joram sent men-at-arms and squads of charioteers as he could spare them from their border posts. But the real defense against Jezebel's harangue was Elisha and his men from the prophets' schools at Jericho, Gilgal, Bethel, and Carmel. They went throughout the land putting down riots, pleading with the people to stand fast for Jehovah, cajoling and threatening them with the laws of the scriptures, praying for a return to obedience to both religious and civil laws.

In many places they were successful in restoring order and a sense of balance for the people. This was especially true where Elisha asked for special signs from Jehovah to show his power to the people. God answered Elisha in dramatic ways. At Jericho, the Lord again purified the waters of the springs with salt. At Gilgal, he purified a deadly pottage. And near Carmel, he led Elisha to instruct a young prophet's widow on how she could use an unspent jar of oil to provide income for herself and her sons.

People began to praise Elisha, thinking that he performed miracles. "It is not I you should thank," he protested. "It is the Lord God Jehovah's power that moves among you. Honor him with your obedience to his laws. Ignore the lure of Jezebel and her false prophets. They bring you nothing but pain and death."

He was right, of course. Merari sat down on a rough wooden bench near the pottery shed. Considering all that happened in the past seven years, the Kingdom of Israel was as evil-ridden as it had been during the reign of Joram's older brother and during the reign of their father, Ahab, before that. Nothing had really changed. Except for pockets of peacefulness and order, like the area around Shunem, disruptions, violence, mistrust, and hunger were abroad in the land. She saw it in her father's eyes each time he returned from his trips to Damascus and Tyre. She sensed it in the frequent, but brief, visits Elisha now made to his room on the wall. She heard it in the rumble of Joram's chariot corps coming and going along the Megiddo road in front of the house. She even saw it in Nahum's eyes whenever one of his men was conscripted for Joram's border patrols.

"Israel has disobeyed the laws of the Lord for many years," Elisha often told them. "The destruction of the royal house is predestined. So is the destruction of the kingdom. The Lord will not be flaunted!"

Merari leaned back against the wall of the pottery shed and with a heavy sigh questioned, "Is all really well?" She left the question unanswered.

By now, day had fully pushed away the canopy of night. The household was stirring. Only the smallest of breezes riffled the leaves of the huge tamarisk next to her. She dabbed again at her forehead with the square of cotton and walked back toward the house to awaken Ozem. She must get him ready for his great adventure of "helping with the work in the fields."

A little over an hour later, she watched him ride along with Tamar on a young donkey toward the nearest fields. "Don't stay too long. It's a very hot day!" she called after them.

Ozem, mimicking Tamar, turned, waved, and nodded his head obediently. Merari lingered, watching them go until she could no longer see them in the distance. Returning to the house, she set about her own chores. She had been at them for only a short while when one of the servants came to tell her that Commander Jehu had arrived and was asking to see her. She put down her mending and went into the main part of the house.

"Commander?"

He turned to acknowledge her greeting, and as he did so, a small face peered around at her.

She grinned in astonishment. The boy could not have been more than eight years of age, with a thin face dominated by enormous dark eyes which questioned with open curiosity. "And who might your young friend be, Commander Jehu?"

Jehu glanced down, and with a laugh pulled the boy around so that Merari could have a full-length view of him. "This is Hakkatan."

"Your son?"

"No, m'lady." His rumbling voice had a touch of tenderness in it. "This lad's father was a close friend of mine who was killed not long ago in a skirmish north of here. The boy is orphaned."

A pang of sorrow went through Merari.

"I'm taking Hakkatan to Samaria. He has an older cousin there who will care for him."

A servant entered carrying refreshments. Both the boy and Jehu accepted Merari's invitation to have some.

She watched them for a moment, thinking what a fine playmate for Ozem the boy Hakkatan might make. Not that Ozem needed any more playmates. He already had a dozen or more. Many of the servants had children near his age. But she wished Ozem was here so he could meet Hakkatan. There was a certain quality about this little boy sitting so quietly beside the burly chariot commander that tugged at her. Of course, arrangements had already been made for his care, and probably Jehu had gone to quite a bit of trouble to arrange it. She must not interfere.

"The reason for my stopping here, m'lady, is to inquire about the holy man."

"Elisha?"

"Yes, m'lady. King Joram told me to find him and tell him that the king needs his advice about the impending war with Syria. King Joram wants his advice."

"I'm pleased that our king seeks such advice," Merari smiled. "But Elisha isn't here. He's at Mount Carmel."

Jehu frowned, disappointed. He glanced at the boy.

"There is a problem, Commander?"

"The problem is a matter of time. Both for the boy and

for me. The boy's cousin travels to Jerusalem the day after tomorrow and wants to take the boy with him. And Joram —that is, the king—has ordered me to take command of the border patrols as soon as I find the holy man and deliver to him the royal message." He reached into his sash and pulled out a narrow scroll. He stared down at it.

"Can I help?"

"Could I leave this with you for the holy man?"

"Of course. Or, if you like, I can send it along to Elisha at Carmel while you and Hakkatan continue to Samaria."

A grateful smile creased his weathered face. "Thank you, m'lady." He handed her the scroll and stood up.

Obediently, the boy stood up, too; but he looked longingly at the food still on the table.

"Would you like to carry some food with you, Commander?"

"Oh no, ma'am. We'll be fine until we reach Samaria."

"For the boy?" she added quietly.

Jehu looked surprised and glanced down at the lad. He grinned at Merari. "A picnic along the way might be nice, after all."

The boy looked up at him and, for the first time, smiled.

Merari motioned for the servant to wrap up the food and carry it to the chariot for them. She followed along, watching the gentle way Jehu tied the boy to the chariot so he wouldn't tumble out during their trip. Such gentleness from such a hard, strong man was unexpected. She felt a new respect for him.

Satisfied that the boy was safely secured, Jehu turned and saluted her. With a shy smile, the boy waved, too; and the chariot went forward.

Merari waved back and watched them move off toward Samaria.

It was by now midmorning. The sun had climbed steadily toward its zenith, blazing its heat earthward. She shielded her eyes against its brilliance and searched the horizon for Tamar and Ozem, wishing they were back. They had been out long enough in this heat. But the horizon appeared empty. No need to worry, she told herself. Tamar was a responsible young woman. And Nahum would not let them stay too long in the fields. Still and all, the day had grown unusually hot. She dabbed at her forehead with the square of cotton. It was too hot to send a servant off to Carmel with the message for Elisha until much later in the day.

Once more, she shielded her eyes against the sun and looked for the returning figures of Tamar and Ozem, but the horizon only shimmered with a worrisome, unwanted emptiness.

Fear-ridden thoughts invaded her consciousness. Where could they be? They had been gone much too long. But what could happen to them? she asked herself rather sternly, trying to shake off the anxiety crowding into her mind. There was no more trusted servant in all the household than Tamar. And Nahum certainly would not let anything harmful occur. He would watch over their son. Even more important, Ozem was in God's power. The Lord would protect him. She knew *that* deep in her heart. Elisha had proclaimed the blessing on the day Ozem was born. Why should she worry? Still, the sense of uneasiness continued to grow inside her.

"All is well." She said the words almost automatically, trying to override her growing concern, trying to fight down the certain feeling that something dreadful already had occurred. It was as if she could hear Ozem crying out in pain. A shaft of fear lanced her heart. She felt sick at the very thought. Pulling the hood of her robe over her head to shield herself from the sun, she went out from the gate to search for him.

She had gone only a short way when she saw Tamar and another servant hurrying toward her from the distance with the little donkey. She stopped dead still.

"All is well," she forced herself to whisper as a prayer of positive protest against whatever had gone wrong. "All is well!" Anxiously she clung to the words in defiance of disaster, determining out of sheer will that danger should not permanently touch her child. Desperate now, she ran toward the approaching figures.

With anguished eyes, she watched as Tamar lifted Ozem down from the little donkey and placed him in her arms.

"The sun, m'lady," Tamar cried. "It has hurt his head!"

Ozem moaned. His face was white, his brow feverish. And yet when she touched his cheek, it was curiously clammy.

"We must get him to someplace cool." Frantically, she cast about for the coolest place in the compound. "The prophet's room," she said. "That will do. Carry him up there."

The manservant took Ozem from her.

"Tamar, go for water. Cool water and some cloths. Lots of cloths!" Hurriedly she followed the servant up the stairs.

Inside the prophet's room, she dismissed the servant and sat down on a stool with Ozem in her lap. Gently, she removed his outer garments and loosened the rest of his clothing. Tamar appeared, along with Achsa, carrying jugs of water and a load of fresh cloths.

Achsa had brought along a small fan also. She began to stir the air around Ozem's small figure. Tamar doused the cloths with water and handed them to Merari to wash down his body. In a silence broken only by an occasional word of reassurance for each other, the women worked over Ozem for a very long time. They worked so long, in fact, that midday arrived, turning the sky coppery with its heat and destroying what small breeze had found its way into the room.

Even so, it appeared that Ozem was better. His body temperature had cooled; his brow was no longer feverish. Achsa stopped using the fan and went out with Tamar to fetch fresh clothing for him. Merari got up and carried him to Elisha's bed. She laid him on it. Then she stood looking down at him for a long time, loving him as never before and thanking the Lord God Jehovah for giving him to her and Nahum, and praising the holy name of the Lord for protecting him from the hated sunstroke. She leaned over to kiss him.

It was then she realized he was no longer breathing.

-10-

An awesome silence hovered in the room. A horrible mistake of nature had occurred. Time's ceaseless journey suspended, as shock seeped into Merari's heart and flooded her with an overwhelming fear.

She sank to the floor beside the bed. Her arms ached from having held Ozem for so long. Absent-mindedly, she rubbed at them, stirring circulation until first one, then the other arm tingled with new life. But Ozem remained motionless, seemingly in peaceful sleep.

She stared at him, wondering if she should cry or scream or wail, or curse the evil which had befallen her and her household. But none of those sounds of defeat and hysteria and release would come. Sorrow, and unspeakable emptiness, overpowered her. Only the deepest part of her soul contradicted the seeming reality before her eyes.

She reached out to touch him, to caress his face with the tips of her fingers. It cannot be. It must not be. It will not be! She cradled her head against the edge of the bed.

Faintly, from the depths of her spirit, a tiny spark of faith rekindled itself, signaling that life-giving power still existed. "Pray," she heard herself say. "Pray for God's great power. Your child is his gift to you."

Tentatively, she raised her head, listening, unsure that the voice she heard was her own. "Pray. There is special power in prayers of praise and thanksgiving. Since the days of Elijah, and before, God has asked his people to pray that way."

She began hesitantly, as if she never before had prayed. "O Lord . . . I praise . . . your holy name." Her voice had a peculiarly distant quality to it. "I thank you, Lord . . . for Ozem. I thank you for his life and for his . . . perfect health. With all my heart, I believe that you gave Ozem to me and Nahum to love and to cherish throughout a long lifetime. I believe only good . . . for him . . . O Lord." Her voice broke as an anguished sob escaped from the well of sorrow deep inside her. "O God, let him live. Let him live!"

The tears came freely now. And as they did, a peculiarly determined resolve filtered through her. It began to fill her unspeakable emptiness. It spoke to her spirit in such a way that she knew what she must now do. She leaned over, kissed her child's forehead, got to her feet, went out of the prophet's room, and carefully closed the door behind her.

At the foot of the stairs, she saw Nahum and the workers coming in from the fields.

He called up to her, "How is Ozem?"

"All is well," she replied firmly.

"He is sleeping?"

She nodded. "Tell Achsa and Tamar not to disturb him, please."

Nahum agreed and started toward the office in the pottery shed.

Merari stopped him and asked him to send her one of the young men with a donkey and a cart so that she might go to Carmel to see Elisha.

Nahum looked puzzled. "Today? In this heat?"

She forced a smile. "It's important. It won't take long. I'll be back before the passing of the day."

"And what about the boy?"

"Leave him be. He was very tired."

"Very well. Don't hurry in this heat." Nahum motioned for one of the workers to bring around a donkey cart, and went on toward the pottery shed.

Merari stepped up into the cart. "Please hurry. Drive as fast as you can. Don't slow down for my comfort unless I tell you to."

The young man nodded and they set off at a fast trot.

Elisha's place at Carmel was located on a north-facing slope of one of the easternmost prominences of the Carmel Mountains. The journey to it from Shunem was not long, maybe three or four miles—five at the most, if the River Kirshon was in flood. At this time of the year, however, the river had barely a trickle of water; and in fact the donkey cart carrying Merari crossed it so quickly that she scarcely recognized it as the river through which the Lord had sent the flood to drown the Baal priests in Elijah's time. "A God as powerful as that is the power of life for Ozem," she encouraged herself.

Immediately ahead, veiled in a curtain of undulating heat waves, the mountains loomed larger and larger. Through the mirage shimmering up from the plain, tawny slopes shouldered up into plateaus of emerald and pink. At any other time, Merari would have wanted to linger over the view, to drink in the beauty and the grandeur of the mountains.

But today all her thoughts were for Ozem. He was alive. *He was alive.* All really *was* well with Ozem. But she must find Elisha. And quickly. And quickly he must come.

The cart driver pointed ahead, over the donkey's bobbing head. A figure was coming toward them at a fast pace. Dust roiling up hid the rider for a moment; then Merari saw that it was Gehazi on one of the horses she had given to him and Elisha. As they drew closer together, the cart driver pulled up to a halt.

Gehazi nodded with great courtesy and dismounted. "My master saw you coming, m'lady. He sent me to greet you and to ask you what the trouble is." He scrutinized the driver, the cart, the donkey pulling it, and finally Merari herself. Apparently unable to find anything wrong, he said, "My master also told me to inquire about your husband and your child."

"Thank you, Gehazi. Your welcome is a warm one. But I came to see your master. Will you show us the way?"

Although he looked disappointed, he remounted his horse without further hesitation, turned around, and led them the rest of the way up the mountain trail to Elisha.

The sight of her friend unnerved her. She jumped from the cart before it rolled to a complete halt and ran toward him.

"Merari!" he exclaimed, startled at her unexpected action. "Is there trouble in Shunem?"

Before she could answer, Gehazi jumped from his horse and rushed to intercept her, as if an interpreter might now required for speaking to his master.

"No, Gehazi!" Elisha roared. "No, let her alone!"

Gehazi backed off, suddenly remembering his place, and motioned for the cart driver to come with him so that Merari could be alone with Elisha.

Elisha waited until he was sure that the servants were out of earshot; then he took Merari's hand. "Something is deeply troubling you, my friend. What is it?"

She looked up at him with pleading eyes, as if she expected him already to know what was wrong.

"I know that something is wrong, Merari. But I don't know what. The Lord has not yet told me what it is. Won't you tell me, that I may help you?"

"It was you who said I would have a son," she reminded him, suddenly finding her voice. "And I begged you not to lie to me."

A look of stupefaction came into his face.

"I begged you. And you reassured me."

"And your child *was* born!"

"To now be taken away?"

He stared at her in silence, his eyes searching every inch of her face and into the depths of her eyes.

"I refuse to believe he has been taken away," she said, barely controlling her emotions. "I will not accept it. Such an act is not the work of the Lord. It cannot be! All *must* be well for Ozem."

Elisha tightened his hold on her hand and looked heavenward in intense concentration. Soon his lips began to move in silent prayer.

Merari went down onto her knees and added her prayers to his. "All is well. All is well." She repeated the phrase over and over, used it to hold back the flood of fear roiling anew inside her.

Elisha gently pulled her back up onto her feet, turned, and called for Gehazi.

The servant instantly appeared from around the corner of a building. Merari's cart driver was right behind him.

"Take my staff, Gehazi, and go quickly to the house of Shunem. Speak to no one on the way. Speak to no one when you arrive. Absolutely no one. Not even to Tamar. Go directly to my room on the wall and lay my staff on the face of the child Ozem."

Gehazi's eyes bulged with astonishment, but he asked no questions. He ran to find Elisha's staff. The cart driver stood stock-still, fear and sorrow intermingled in his eyes.

"All will be well, Merari," Elisha reassured her, leading her back to her cart.

She resisted with a shake of her head.

"Please, Merari," Elisha insisted. "Believe me, all will be well."

Still she refused. "I swear to God that I won't go home without you, Elisha. I simply will not do it. I came to fetch *you* for my son, not Gehazi. I have prayed, too. It's you, Elisha, who is to come with me!"

His eyes widened, and with only another moment's hesitation he relented.

Gehazi went on ahead to lay the staff upon Ozem's face as Elisha had instructed, then hurried back to meet them on the road as the cart approached the house.

"Well?" Elisha asked.

Gehazi shook his head. "The child is dead, master. He is cold."

"He is not dead," Merari said, "He is *not* dead. I will not accept it. All is well."

- 112 -

The young cart driver looked at her with pity.

Elisha tapped him on the shoulder and motioned for him to go forward once again. When they arrived at the house, Elisha went directly to the room on the wall; and there he found Ozem lying dead upon his bed.

He went in and shut the door and prayed to the Lord. Then he lay upon the child's body, placing his mouth upon the child's mouth, and his eyes upon the child's eyes, and his hands upon the child's hands. And the child's body began to grow warm again.

Then Elisha went down and walked back and forth within the compound. He spoke to no one. Not to Merari. Not even to Nahum. To no one. By this time, the people of the household crowded about, watching him with anxious faces and nervous eyes. Apart from the others, Merari and Nahum sat together holding hands, but not daring to look at each other. Fear and sorrow etched twin furrows in Nahum's face. The pallor of dejection was visible beneath the weathered tan of his face. From time to time, they closed their eyes and their lips moved in silent prayer. Elisha stood for a time watching them, praying in his own way. Finally, he turned and went back up the stairs to his room.

Once again, he stretched himself upon the child.

This time, the boy sneezed seven times and then, opened his eyes!

Elisha arose, went to the door, and called down to Gehazi who was waiting at the bottom of the stairs. "My servant, call Merari and Nahum. Ask them to come here."

When they stepped through the doorway, Elisha met them, looked deeply into their faces, and said very gently, "Your prayers are answered. Your faith is fulfilled. Through God's power, your son lives."

"Mother? Father?" Ozem smiled up at them from behind the folds of Elisha's robes.

Nahum dropped to his knees, hugged the boy to his chest, and wept.

Merari stood silently watching, relief and gratitude over-whelming her. "Thank you, Lord. I praise your holy name."

Reaction to the miracle of resurrection came swiftly from the people of the household gathered in the courtyard. With their eyes, they had followed Merari and Nahum up the stairs and into the room of the prophet; then they waited in a tense, questioning silence. When the couple reap-peared, with a squirming Ozem in Nahum's arms, the awe-struck household murmured in astonishment.

Achsa and Tamar stepped forward tentatively to question Elisha, who watched from the top of the stairs.

"It is as your mistress said all along," Elisha called down to them. "All is well!"

Tears of joy sprang into the eyes of the old nurse.

Tamar sank down onto her knees and wept in relief.

Gehazi hurried to her and put his arms around her.

Two of the field workers left the courtyard and ran to-ward Shunem to report the miracle there.

The crowd's murmur of astonishment exploded into shouts of rejoicing. As the full realization came that the power of God had moved through Elisha, and into the very being of the boy, they began to sing and dance and shout their praises to the one true God Jehovah.

-11-

It was not until much later, in the deepest hours of the night, that Merari remembered the summons brought by Jehu for Elisha.

She awakened Nahum and told him about it. He got up, pulled a robe around him, and took the message up to the prophet's room. Elisha read it immediately and decided to go at once to Samaria.

The sudden departure gave Gehazi no chance to say good bye to Tamar. All during the journey he did little to conceal his injured feelings. "Marriage is much on my mind, master," he had retorted when Elisha finally asked what the trouble was. "Walking out on Tamar without so much as a word is scarcely a way to woo her."

Elisha laughingly teased him. "How would you support a wife? Even if she would have you?"

Gehazi found no humor in the question. "We had much to talk about. Especially after the miracle you wrought with the boy."

"*I* wrought no miracle. That was the Lord's doing."

"You were his instrument, master. Tamar was still feeling guilty about not watching Ozem carefully enough when they were in the fields. I was trying to console her."

"I'm sorry, Gehazi," Elisha said with compassion. "But the king's need for counsel is urgent. Ben-Hadad of Damascus and the King of Syria both are sorely menacing Israel now."

"There is nothing new in that," Gehazi muttered, half to himself.

"But Joram sees this menace as more threatening than all

the others. Joram sees a serious war threatening."

"Why is it, master, that you always go to the king's aid in these matters? You know he doesn't believe in the Lord God Jehovah."

Elisha gave the servant a sharp look, surprised at this apparent lack of understanding. "Loyalty to the kingdom against all outsiders should not be a hard thing to understand. The worship of false gods comes in many forms. No matter how severe our disagreements inside the kingdom, we must work together against all outside threats, Gehazi. You know that. You've heard me say it often enough. That's why I counsel with Joram whenever he asks. The Lord God has instructed me to do it."

Gehazi subsided into a fretful silence that continued until they reached the outer gates of the Ivory Palace in the city of Samaria. Not until the sentry atop the gate saluted them, and they had reined their horses to a stop, did he find his voice. Then, as if suddenly wanting recognition for the importance of his own role as servant to Elisha, Gehazi stood up in his stirrups and shouted to the sentry, "My master, the prophet Elisha, comes in answer to the summons of your King Joram!"

Almost immediately, the gates swung open, allowing them to enter. Obadiah came toward them from a private doorway at the far end of the entry veranda. Gehazi jumped from his horse to attend Elisha with a great show of respect before the palace grooms appeared.

"Greetings, Honorable Prophet," Obadiah bowed. "Our thanks to you for coming."

Elisha saluted in return, feeling once again the familiar sense of security in the presence of this wise old man who for so many years had provided balance and reason to the royal courts of Israel. Nahum was fortunate to have him as an uncle. "I bring you greetings from Shunem, sir."

Obadiah's eyes wrinkled into a smile. "Then it is well with my loved ones, Merari and Nahum?"

Elisha nodded.

"And what of that fine young lad, my great-nephew? Is it well with Ozem, too?"

"Aye, it is well."

"*Now* it is well with Ozem," Gehazi muttered.

Both men turned in surprise—Obadiah startled and curious, Elisha with a disapproving frown.

Obadiah turned again to Elisha. "What does he mean? Has something happened to Ozem?"

Before Elisha could form the words, Gehazi, eyes wide with wonder at the recollection of it, blurted out the whole miraculous story. He told of Ozem's illness, the death, the summoning of Elisha by Merari, the hurried journey to Shunem, the resurrection. His words tumbled out in a spate of excitement. When he finished, triumphant and breathless, Obadiah looked from the servant to the prophet with consternation.

"The boy is well," Elisha said reassuringly.

"And Merari came for you?" the old man questioned.

Elisha nodded. "It was Merari's unquestioning faith that allowed the power of God to prevail."

Obadiah relaxed a bit.

"Never at any time did she confess that Ozem was dead. Never once, during the whole ordeal, did she claim such a defeat with words. She kept her own counsel. Even when she came to get me, she was acting in faith. It was not until Gehazi met us in the roadway with the report of Ozem's death that I fully understood just how much she was acting in faith. Her spirit had spoken to my spirit of some trouble. But her words had never revealed its exact nature."

"What did she say to you?"

"She simply said, 'All is well,' in response to my questions."

"All is well?" Obadiah repeated. His eyes reflected disbelief as he led the way to Joram's counsel chambers.

Elisha motioned for Gehazi to stay with the horses. "Merari's very words described her unrelenting faith. The words manifested her absolute refusal to accept the death of the boy."

Obadiah glanced at him sidewise. "Are you telling me that Merari's use of certain words gives her power others of us don't have?"

Elisha shook his head. "I'm telling you that because she refused to accept death for her son, she allowed the power of God—the power of life—to work through me for the resurrection of the boy's flesh."

Obadiah fell silent, pondering this as a new possibility of life.

Elisha walked beside him, welcoming the older man's search for a yet deeper truth. Wise as Obadiah was, most of his wisdom dealt with things of the physical world. His association with Ahab and Jezebel, and now with Joram, allowed for precious little else. But he had a perceptive soul; and his love for Nahum, Merari, and the boy, if nothing else, would cause him to open his mind. For in truth, Merari had activated a deep spiritual reality. Faith, like love, is always shown in actions. And Merari's actions clearly were the evidence of her faith.

Finally Obadiah broke the silence. "What about Nahum? Was his faith as strong as Merari's?"

Elisha shook his head. "Nahum's faith was not tested in the same way. He knew only that the boy had stayed too long in the sun. When he cried, 'My head, my head,' Nahum told the servants to take him to his mother. But he knew nothing more."

"Why was that?"

"Because when he and his men returned from the fields and he asked about the boy, Merari simply said, 'All is well.' Nahum accepted her word and went on about the business of the day."

Obadiah looked at the prophet in astonishment. "Then Nahum never knew the boy had died?"

Elisha smiled and shook his head. "Merari admitted the boy's death to no one. Not even to herself!"

By this time, they had reached the door to Joram's counsel chamber. Two sentries came to attention.

Obadiah stopped just out of their hearing and faced the prophet with a direct look. "Did the boy *really* die?"

"Do you doubt the ability of human faith to influence God's power?"

Obadiah did not answer.

"Do you doubt the power of God?"

Still Obadiah made no answer, but a tinge of color rose in his face and magnified the pondering look deep in his eyes.

Elisha smiled and grasped the older man's arm. "Believe that all is well with your loved ones in Shunem. Now, as never before, all is well with them."

Obadiah relented a bit. "All the same, let us not discuss this with Joram. His mind is on other things. I want nothing to distract him from the power of your prophecies for the kingdom. Nor do I want him to doubt you more than he already does."

"I understand," Elisha laughed and followed the old minister through the doorway and into the counsel chambers.

Joram stood looking at a large map drawn on an animal hide and tacked unceremoniously on the far wall. Depicted on the map were the positions of Ben-Hadad's latest forays along Israel's northeastern border. At the upper portion of the map a series of X's, connected by dotted lines, showed the path of movement of the Syrian forces. They converged with yet a third line, representing Ben-Hadad's anticipated advance, and rendezvous point with Syria.

"Famine and drouth, disease and destruction," Elisha said almost to himself as he went across the room to study the map more closely.

Joram heard him and swung around. "Say it again, Prophet. Loudly enough for me to hear it clearly."

Elisha ignored the measured stare, the threatening tone, and continued to study the crude map.

"What do you see that I don't see?"

"You are the warrior," Elisha said easily. "The map

should tell you all that is necessary, shouldn't it?"

Joram gave a hard laugh, walked to a nearby table where a carafe of wine and some cups were sitting, and poured wine for them all. Elisha took the offered wine cup and raised it in salute to both Obadiah and Joram.

"Your god must have bad news for me," Joram said. "When you answer my questions with questions, it usually means your god wants something I don't."

"But when you listen to Jehovah and do what he wants, you're successful," Elisha countered. "Beginning with your defeat of Mesha of Moab when you first became king."

"I had a good ally then."

"Indeed you did. Jehoshaphat was Jehovah's man."

"I have no ally in Judah, now that Jehoshaphat is dead." He glanced sharply toward Obadiah. "My adviser keeps telling me that Benaiah and the others will soon persuade Jehoram of Judah to help me against Ben-Hadad and the Syrians. I don't believe it."

"No, sire. That's not what I've been telling you," Obadiah quickly contradicted. "What I've been saying is that we should not *want* Jehoram of Judah's allegiance. He has made one blunder after another. He has violated all the treaties his father put in place. He would be of no help to us. He would turn on us if it suited him and go to war against us if he could."

"Obadiah is right," Elisha agreed. "Jehoram of Judah has defied all of God's warnings. He would be of no help to you."

Joram gave them both a wary look. "Do you give counsel, Prophet, to Jehoram, too?"

Elisha set aside the wine cup and wiped at his beard. "Jehoram has never sought my advice."

Joram's expression did not change. He walked toward a large, handsomely carved chair and sat down. "Well then, tell me what advice you bring to me. Will there be war with Syria soon?"

Elisha shook his head. "Not in the way that you think."

"What does that mean?"

Elisha walked to the map and pointed at the route Joram was expecting the Syrians to take. "Your anticipation of what the Syrians will do is wrong. Eager as he is for battle with you, the King of Syria will not commit a strong force yet."

"Why not?"

"The famine will stop him."

"What famine?"

"Here. And here." Elisha punched at the map with his forefinger at two places near Israel's northern border where skirmishes with Ben-Hadad's raiders had been the heaviest. "It has already started."

Joram rose from the chair and joined him at the map. "I've had no reports of it."

"It's caused by a drouth."

"I have no reports of that either."

"No matter. It's creeping across all the land of Israel. It will last seven years, affecting even the most productive parts of Israel. Even the great Plain of Jezreel."

"Even there?"

Elisha nodded, watching Joram carefully. He reminded himself that in all the excitement to restore the breath of life to Ozem, he had failed to tell Merari and Nahum of the coming drouth and famine. He must warn them. Even before Merari had come for him at Carmel, the Lord had told him to warn the Shunem family, and to encourage them to leave the land.

"Seven years?" Joram asked. "You're wrong, Prophet. You must be. There has never been a drouth of such long duration. Not in the history of the kingdom. Even in Elijah's time, the drouth endured for only three years."

Elisha shrugged and turned to look across the room at Obadiah. Sadness filled the face of the old minister. It was as if he, too, had shared the revelation from Jehovah about his beloved nation, as if he had a premonition of its ultimate fate.

"Disobedience to the laws of Jehovah profits us little," Obadiah said in a low tone.

Joram wheeled about in anger. "What disobedience? Did I not tear down the altar and the pillar of Baal here at the palace? Have I not quelled every riot the idolators have started? Have I not encouraged you, Elisha, and the men from your prophets' schools to disavow every preaching of Jezebel's priests?"

"You have."

"What more can I do? What will appease this god of yours?"

"There is still sin in the land, sire." Obadiah put in.

"Am I responsible for every fornication that happens?"

"Perhaps you are," Elisha said. "As a man, you are responsible for your own sins. None more. But as king, you are responsible for setting an example of obedience to God's laws for the people of your nation."

"What rot!" Joram turned away, paced to the far part of the counsel chamber, and stared out into his private courtyard.

Elisha followed him. "You could put a stop to Jezebel's constant practices of evil."

Joram stiffened. A muscle in his jaw flexed.

"You could rid the land of her Baal-worshiping priests."

"She would never allow it."

"Then you should rid the land of Jezebel!"

Obadiah's gasp of astonishment came audibly across the room.

Joram flinched as if struck. "She's my mother!"

"As long as you allow her the freedom to practice evil, you and your nation will pay for it."

Joram turned away, as if the physical act would somehow revoke everything he had just heard.

"Exile Jezebel." Elisha pursued. "Rid the land of her and her followers. Otherwise, famine and drouth, disease and destruction will fall on all of Israel."

Joram walked back to the table on which the carafe was sitting and poured more wine into his cup.

Elisha followed him. "Jehovah is very clear in his commandments to us. Since the time of Moses, the first law has been, 'Thou shalt have no other gods before me.' That is still Jehovah's law. Your mother constantly violates it. And so do you."

"But I don't believe in her gods. Or in yours!"

"Then why summon me? Why seek my counsel?"

Joram stood perfectly still, as if frozen. He seemed scarcely to breathe. Whatever was going through his mind remained strictly within him. Heavy silence hovered for seconds, then minutes; still he made no response.

Finally Elisha broke the silence. "This is the revelation given me by the Lord God Jehovah for you, King Joram of Israel. There will be famine and drouth, disease and destruction throughout the land for seven years."

Still there was no response from Joram.

Elisha glanced toward Obadiah.

"Elisha has always given you accurate predictions in times past, sire."

Slowly, Joram turned toward them. Sadness etched his face, making him seem older than he really was. In a faraway voice he said, "She is my mother, Obadiah. Bad as she is, she is still my mother. I will not exile her. As for you, Elisha, your words are no comfort to me. Your predictions, while they may be true, are of no value to me. You may leave whenever you wish. Or you may stay as a guest in my palace for a few days. Obadiah will see to your needs." He turned, walked to a side door, and disappeared through it.

Elisha sighed in disappointment.

Obadiah came to him. "What other reaction could you expect? You're right, of course. Jezebel should be exiled. But you should know that even though Joram defies her in many ways, and controls her activities more than anyone thought he could, he stops short of really dominating her. No one dominates Jezebel!"

- 123 -

"Then Israel is doomed, old friend. The Lord God Jehovah will not be flaunted." A sudden tiredness overwhelmed him. He realized how little rest he'd had since the revival of Ozem. And that act had taken from him an enormous amount of energy. He went to a nearby chair, sat down, and stared at the floor while concentrating to refresh his energy level.

Obadiah misread his actions. "Don't feel you're defeated yet, Elisha. Let me talk further with Joram. He doesn't yet know of the miracle wrought through you for Ozem. Once he learns of it, he may be persuaded to give greater credence to your words. Stay and rest here for a day or two. Let me speak with him further."

If there appeared to be no victory for Elisha in his confrontation with Joram, exactly the opposite was true for his servant. Gehazi found himself the center of attention because of the resurrection of Ozem. News of the miracle had traveled fast and far through a miracle of its own—word of mouth. From field hands and Shunem household servants to caravan men to soldiers to charioteers to servants in the Ivory Palace in Samaria, the news was passed and received with wide-eyed astonishment. Not since the great prophet Elijah revived the son of the widow of Zarephath many years before had such a wondrous event occurred in the Kingdom of Israel. It was a manifestation of the power of the Lord God Jehovah which could not be duplicated by any of the gods of Baal. And now the appearance of the servant of the prophet who had wrought the miracle was a great and an unexpected event.

Palace guards listening to Gehazi tell of the wondrous occurrence were joined by people from the city itself—tradesmen, merchants, householders, and artisans—and by visitors from other cities in the kingdom. One rather well-dressed courier from Jezreel seemed particularly interested. He joined the others swarming around Gehazi like bees around blossoms to hear the miraculous story.

Gehazi told it well. And truthfully. But when questions

came from the crowd, and particularly from the well-dressed courier, he grew less modest about his own role in the matter.

"It even seemed possible, Your Majesty," the same well-dressed courier reported to Jezebel on his return to her palace in the city of Jezreel, "that the servant Gehazi would gladly have taken all credit for the resurrection for himself. His modesty was quite thin by the time the crowd broke up."

A cynical smile played across Jezebel's face. Her hands toyed with a tassel of the cincture at her waist. Her eyes probed the courier's face. "You say the resurrection of the Shunammite's child occurred only recently?"

"Within just a few days past, apparently."

"Do you believe such a thing can be true?"

The courier hesitated.

"Well, do you?"

"It does seem that—"

"Do you believe that it really happened?" she insisted.

"Yes, Your Majesty," came the reluctant reply.

Jezebel's probing look flickered briefly. "And what about the people in the crowd with you? Did they believe it?"

Again the courier hesitated.

"Well, did they?"

"I think so, Your Majesty. Yes, I think most of them did." He shuffled uncomfortably from one foot to the other.

"And what of the king?" She knew better than to ask. It was a needless question. For some time she had been aware of Joram's frequent requests for advice from Elisha. He not only asked for advice; he took it, as well. Of course he would believe such a story. He might even believe in the god they called Jehovah! "Does he believe this thing occurred?"

"He didn't at first, Your Majesty."

"What do you mean, 'Not at first'?"

"The king didn't believe it at all until he went to Shunem to see for himself that the child is alive."

Surprise jolted her. "To Shunem?"

"Yes, Your Majesty. King Joram took the prophet and his servant, and the Master of the Royal Palaces, the Honorable Obadiah, with him."

"And is the child alive?"

"Very much alive. He was quite excited about seeing his great Uncle Obadiah, and his friend, the prophet. There was a fine celebration going on at the house in Shunem, I am told."

With an impatient wave of her hand, she dismissed him. She stood up and walked to the latticed window that overlooked the street below. People were everywhere. Coming and going. All sorts and kinds. All subject to the will of the King of Israel. Her son! The son who had never wanted to be king. The son she could never trust to do her bidding. The son who had destroyed her favorite place of worship. The son who sought advice from a prophet who could resurrect dead boys. "Fools!" she muttered to herself. "No one can be brought back to life. The boy was never dead. Only fools would believe he was."

She turned away from the window, irritated by the thought that great numbers of people would believe that a miracle had occurred, angered by the effect she knew the occurrence would have on the worship of Baal and the amount of tribute paid to Baal. It would affect her personal wealth and her influence as leader of the nation's Baal worshipers. "Such fools!"

An effort would have to be made to prove to all of them that the power of Baal was even greater than the power claimed for Jehovah. But what should that effort be? She paced back and forth, considering several possibilities. Whichever one she chose, she was determined that it would make an indelible imprint on the minds of those who dared to believe that Jehovah was more powerful than Baal. Regardless of who they were, or what their station in life, they would learn in time that she, as Baal's personal representative, was just as powerful as the bald prophet called Elisha.

- 12 -

Seldom had the house in Shunem been in such an uproar as it was in the aftermath of Ozem's miraculous resurrection. The villagers of Shunem put on a great feast of celebration. Then for weeks after that, passersby continued to stop in, wanting to see the little boy who had been brought back to life. Joram and Obadiah were among them.

The intrusions disrupted preparations for harvest. Welcome as Uncle Obadiah was when he decided to stay on for a while rather than return to Samaria with Joram, his presence added to the household chores and reduced the number of servants who could go to work in the fields. Then Benaiah returned from his most recent diplomatic tour. He was concerned and despondent over Israel's crumbling relations with some of its oldest allies, and his mood added a new dimension of stress to the busy days. Elisha stayed over for several days to counsel with Benaiah about the implications of the Lord's revelations about famine and drouth, disease and destruction. And of course, Gehazi stayed. In the process, he asked Tamar to marry him, which meant there would be a wedding to plan and to hold.

And on top of all else, Elisha repeatedly pressured Nahum and Merari to leave Shunem in order to avoid the prophesied drouth and famine.

"You're already on shaky ground with Joram," he warned Nahum. "Just because he hasn't said anything directly about your conditional appointment, he hasn't forgotten. If your fields don't yield what they have in the past —and they cannot in the forthcoming drouth—he will throw you out as Royal Overseer. He may even confiscate the properties you own, as well. Then where will you be?"

When they appeared to resist his advice, he reminded them, "You have more to think of now than just yourselves. There is the boy to be considered. The Lord didn't resuscitate him without reason. He now belongs to the Lord. At some point, he will have to make his own decision about being a man of God. But while he's still so young, it's your responsibility to keep him as safe as possible. Take my advice, my friends. Leave Shunem."

In only a short period, major changes in their lives were becoming swift reality. It was as if they were being called upon to justify the blessings of life, and to confirm recognition of their responsibility to a greater power.

At last alone in their own rooms after another long, harried day, they wondered over the changes being thrust on them, talked long over whether or not they should move.

"The move will be harder on you, Nahum, than on the rest of us," Merari said in firm practicality.

"Why?"

"Because you will leave your work here. The fields and vineyards and orchards can't be packed up and carried with us."

He laughed quietly. "I suppose not."

"What will you do?" she asked.

He thought for a moment, then teased, "I shall play with my son each day, and make love to my wife each night. *That* will keep me occupied."

"Be serious!"

"I am being serious," he protested. "A prolonged visit with your mother's people in Philistia will be good for both of us. As much as we love this place here in Shunem, it demands much labor from us. I have begun to notice it lately. I tire more easily. "I'm getting old, my wife. Hadn't you noticed?"

She frowned, not liking to think about it. Nahum at leisure seemed such an alien idea.

"It will be good to have a bit less work to do and a bit more time to spend together in other pursuits."

"For a short while, yes, it will be pleasant. But Elisha says the drouth and the famine will last seven years. Can we take so much leisure? Will you be satisfied with that, my husband?"

He turned fully toward her, slipped one arm under her head and cradled her to him. "No, I won't. And that's why I plan to make regular trips back here. I will check on our own lands; and I will check on Joram's land. I will continue to fulfill my Overseer's duties, but conditionally, just as his appointment was conditional."

"But who will look after them when you aren't here?"

"Uncle Obadiah has some trusted friends he can assign here in my absence. And Elisha, too."

"You mean Uncle Obadiah isn't coming with us to Joppa?"

"No. And neither is your father. Except to visit. They will not abandon Joram. They dare not leave him and the nation totally alone with Jezebel and her followers."

Merari shrugged out of Nahum's arms and sat up.

"It will be all right, my beloved. They are wise men."

"But even wise men can starve."

"Starve? In the king's palace? Come, come, Merari. You are more practical than that!"

She was silent for several moments, thinking how great the changes in their lives really would be, envisioning the sadness of separation from things and places familiar, and imagining the heartbreak of being separated from the people she loved. Quietly, she began to cry.

Nahum sat up, put his arms around her, and held her close until she cried away the tension and the frustrations of deep and unwanted changes.

For the next several days, they planned seriously for the move to Joppa. Since they couldn't take with them all who worked for them, and because they wished to cause no panic, they spoke of the trip merely as a visit to Merari's relatives, explaining that since her mother was already there on another of her many visits to her sister, this was the best time for the rest of the family to go.

Tamar couldn't go since she would soon be marrying Gehazi. And Elisha carefully avoided any hint of the real duration of the journey to his servant. That left only Achsa, the nurse, and Kallai to go along to attend them. Neither servant had family nor spouse, but they were told the true reason for the trip in the event they might wish to remain in Shunem with friends. Neither did.

The drovers, herdsmen, and porters who would make the journey would be sent back to Shunem quickly, and would bring with them goods and foodstuffs for those left behind.

All that remained to be decided was a departure date. Elisha, Benaiah, and even Obadiah urged an immediate departure. But Nahum firmly insisted that they wait until the barley harvest was finished. "It will be only a matter of a few days," he said. "We'll start the journey then. Shall we send a courier to Zibia in Joppa?"

And so the departure day was set according to his wishes, and the courier took the news to Zibia. Departure and most of the traveling was planned for nighttime, because it was cooler then . . . at least until the coastal plains were reached.

The day on which the journey was to begin dawned sultry and sullen. The sun appeared as an angry red eye of heaven. Before the third hour of the morning, a hot, dry wind started blowing across the Plain of Jezreel from southeast to northwest. By the ninth hour, its incessant, intrusive blustering had added to the tensions growing within all of them.

Kallai, normally patient with servants who were below his own station and subject to his order, snapped and fussed at the porters and drovers over the loading of the pack animals. Achsa, who never raised her voice, let alone her hand, slapped Ozem's hands as he repeatedly grabbed toys out of the bag a young serving girl was trying to pack. He cried out in surprise and complained loudly to his mother.

Merari was unsympathetic. "You deserved it, Ozem. You know better than to tease like that." She turned to Nahum, who had just come in from the stables and was standing in the doorway observing the scene. "All this attention he's been getting lately is spoiling him."

"Then perhaps the trip will be good in more ways than we thought."

"Perhaps."

"Come with me, Ozem. You're a distraction."

"What's a distraction?" the boy asked.

"Troublesome, lad. Troublesome, like you!" Nahum swung him high in the air and gave him a gentle shaking. The boy laughed, already forgetting the unusual behavior of his nurse, his mother's unsympathetic attitude, and the unfamiliar packing activities. Nahum set him back on his feet. "Let's go pester your grandfather and your uncle for a while," Within a matter of moments, though, they were back. Nahum called for Merari to come with them.

"What's the trouble now?"

"No trouble. A surprise visitor."

"Not Joram again?"

"No, no," Nahum chuckled. "But close. It's Jehu!"

They went out from the private part of the house toward the main salon, where Jehu appeared to be in earnest conversation with Benaiah and Obadiah. As they drew nearer, Merari heard him mention Jezebel and child sacrifice. A chill of fear ran through her. Then she noticed that Jehu had not come alone. He had the little orphan boy, Hakkatan, with him.

"I'm told that Jezebel was livid when she learned of the resurrection of your child," Jehu went on. "At first she claimed it to be a monstrous lie, of course—one devised to elevate the influence of the prophet Elisha. Then, when so many reports continued to come from her own followers, she sent a spy to this very house to see if the child is, in fact, alive."

"And was the spy satisfied that he is?" Nahum asked,

walking into the room with Ozem holding Ozem by the hand and followed by Merari.

Jehu turned and bowed.

Hakkatan and Ozem exchanged shy stares of curiosity and surprise.

"And did the spy report to Jezebel that the boy is alive?" Nahum insisted.

"Yes, my friend. He reported it true."

"Then what happened?" Obadiah prompted.

"Jezebel is now claiming that the event has so enraged Baal, and all the other gods and goddesses, that they will cause famine and drouth, disease and destruction to come on the land."

Benaiah swore. "What else does that despicable whore claim?"

"She also claims that only a very special and very unusual sacrifice will appease Baal and all the other gods and turn away the drouth and the famine."

"And what might that sacrifice be?" Merari heard herself ask in a strangely distant voice.

Jehu turned, looking carefully at her. "Child sacrifice, m'lady. Six orphans. Boys like Hakkatan here. And boys near the age and size of your son!"

- 13 -

The small, private caravan from Shunem forded the River Kanah and crested a final small rise in the Plain of Sharon. In front of them, across an invisible line, lay the wide, green Plain of Philistia like a welcome mat to Joppa. The city was situated atop a high prominence jutting westward into the sea. Early morning dew glistened on the lush foreground. The white and buff buildings of the city shimmered golden in the freshness of the new day against a backdrop of emerald and cobalt.

Mesmerized, they took in the scene, from green foreground to cobalt sea and back again, imprinting on their memory the beauty and peace of this new place. It was to be their home now. Perhaps for a few months. Perhaps for seven years. Perhaps forever.

Only Nahum turned to look back once more, as he had done all through the journey, as if somehow in looking back he could maintain the tie to the house in Shunem and to the land in the Plain of Jezreel.

Merari, and the two little boys clinging to her hands, continued to feast their eyes on what lay before them.

"Ships, Mother. Ships!" Ozem called, pointing to Joppa's small, natural harbor where the masts of many ships could be seen.

"Let's get closer. Let's go!" Hakkatan said excitedly, trying to pull away.

But Merari's hold on both of them was firm.

Nahum laughed. "There'll be time for that later, boys."

"First we must find your Aunt Ilia's house," Merari said. "Your grandmother is waiting for us."

Hakkatan looked over at Ozem, then stared up at Merari. A puzzled look came into his eyes. "Will *my* aunt and grandmother be there, too?"

The question caught Merari by surprise. The boy had no relatives. The one cousin Jehu originally had taken him to be with had been conscripted for the border wars and then killed, leaving the boy alone. Jehu liked him and wanted to keep him, but the danger from Jezebel's crazed threat of further child sacrifice made that impossible. When he had brought Hakkatan to Shunem, she and Nahum had agreed at once to take him into their home for as long as might be necessary. He had fit in so quickly that they had already opened their hearts to him, as well. It seemed quite natural to have him as a part of the family. So natural, in fact, that she had never even given a thought to the idea that Hakkatan might somehow feel strangely out of place.

Ozem abruptly pulled away from her, went to Hakkatan, and put his arm around his shoulder. "They can be your aunt and grandmother, too."

"Suppose they don't like me?"

"*I* like you. Why shouldn't they?"

Hakkatan shrugged.

Nahum came close, stooped, and lifted the orphan in strong arms until they were eye to eye. "We need you, Hakkatan. Ozem's mother and I are so much older than he is that we don't make good playmates. Sometimes we're too busy. Sometimes we're too tired."

The little boy frowned in concentration.

"What we really need is a lad like you. You're about the same size. About the same age. And you seem to like each other. You make a good playmate for Ozem. And he makes a good playmate for you. Almost like brothers."

A light danced in the child's eyes. "Brothers?"

"That's the way it can be, if you want it."

"Then you'd be my relatives?"

"Your family," Nahum agreed.

"The aunt and grandmother, too?"

"The aunt and grandmother, too," Nahum laughed, carrying the boy back to his horse and putting him on it. He turned to help Ozem and Merari remount before climbing on his own horse and giving the signal for the caravan to move forward once again.

The city was as interesting as the approach to it had been impressive. Less than one hundred leagues west of Jerusalem, it was an active, vital port, and had been since the days of King Solomon. Of course, it was a much older city even than that, Merari reminded herself. "The People of the Sea" had settled it so long before that its origin was lost in a forgotten and distant past.

Even so, it still ranked in importance with Tyre, Sidon, and Acre. Great rafts of cedar logs from the forests of Lebanon were floated down the coastline and docked here. Later they were sent on to Judah and to other southern reaches—Egypt, Nubia, Sheba. And after all the years they'd spent in the vast and peaceful silences of the Plain of Jezreel, Joppa was an exciting place. Her mother had been born here. As a child, Merari herself had been brought here on visits many times.

Seeing the place again evoked a twinge of nostalgia. She glanced toward the two youngsters riding between her and Nahum. They said nothing, so filled were they with the sights and sounds of so much activity. Their eyes were bright and shining with the excitement of the crowded, noisy streets. Vendors were everywhere, hawking their wares. It was like a street fair, with sailors rubbing elbows with cameleers, merchants clutching their money pouches to keep them safe from the deft hands of pickpockets, and mothers herding young children quickly past dirty, ragged beggars.

Shoemakers' and leatherworkers' shops sat adjacent to candymakers and weavers. An iron-smelter's shed was across the way from a butcher's shop where goat, sheep, and beef sides hung from great iron hooks.

The caravan continued to make its way through a number

of the busier streets, sometimes slowing almost to a stop, always moving forward once again, until at last they came to a wider street where the crowds seemed to be smaller and where the fresh breeze of salt air assailed them.

"To the left here," Merari called out to the lead drover. "This is the Street of the Shipbuilders." She turned to look at Nahum. "Aunt Ilia's house is only a short distance now. At the top of the incline, overlooking the sea. Remember?"

He nodded and grinned.

She straightened in the saddle. Now she could see one side of Aunt Ilia's house rising straight and white into the morning's brightness. Her pulse quickened. Within a minute, she shouted for the lead drover to turn in at an imposing gateway, and in yet another few seconds, they were all being greeted with squeals and shouts of love and joy from Aunt Ilia's entire household.

Zibia, with a wave of her hand in Merari and Nahum's direction, rushed straight to Ozem, helped him slide from his horse, and began hugging and kissing and hugging him again.

Aunt Ilia made just as directly and just as lovingly for Merari.

Nahum dismounted, went to Hakkatan, lifted him off the horse, and stood close beside him with a protective hand on his shoulder until he could be introduced to the family. He felt the boy tremble and hugged him closer. "It's all right. These are loving people. They will love you. Have no fear, my son."

Zibia spotted them and came toward them.

"This is Hakkatan, little mother. He's new to our household—from Megiddo and Samaria."

"He's my brother, grandmother," Ozem announced.

"How lovely." Zibia smiled, holding out her arms to Hakkatan. "I've always wanted two grandsons."

- 14 -

By the time Joram discovered that Merari, Nahum, and Ozem were no longer full-time residents of the land, almost four years had come and gone. It seemed incredible that that much time could have passed without his learning of the move. The pressures of his role as king had insulated him from that fact. It wasn't that Joram had suddenly stopped thinking about them, or inquiring about them in a general way. Merari was seldom out of his mind. And in his deepest fantasies, he still dreamed of having her as his queen. Rather, it was that the welfare of his nation almost totally absorbed his attention.

He traveled almost constantly: fighting lengthy border skirmishes, counseling with tribal chieftains in the east and to the south, accepting time-consuming ceremonial invitations from heads of other nations in desperate efforts to keep alliances intact.

The drouth had come, as Elisha had predicted. Famine slowly and tenaciously spread throughout the kingdom. Imports were vital to keep some part of Israel's people and economy alive. In this, Benaiah was invaluable and often traveled with Joram on trade missions. Their conversations about personal matters, however, seldom amountd to more than a polite inquiry on Joram's part about the general well-being of the Shunem family. For his part, Benaiah always responded cordially, but never in detail, for he carried a constant worry that if Joram learned of the move, he would do something foolish. Elisha, Obadiah, and Jehu shared his concern and were equally discreet whenever Joram brought up the subject of Shunem or the family.

Occurrences in another area of Joram's life had helped to shield the Shunem move, too. Those occurrences had to do with Jezebel. After learning of her hideous plan to sacrifice six orphan boys, he imprisoned her in her own palace in Jezreel. He threw out her Baal priests. He replaced her palace guards with trusted men of his own. He exiled all of her Baal-worshiping attendants, men and women, except for two eunuchs who were secretly loyal to him.

In almost four years, Jezebel had not been outside the grounds of her palace. Her only communication with the outside world was her letters to Joram and to Athaliah in Jerusalem. At times, Joram regretted that he had given her even that small liberty, for she deluged him with a constant stream of epithets and threatening messages. He ignored most of them; but on occasion, his patience thinned, and he let her messages upset him. Strangely, when that happened Elisha always seemed to be at hand. He took advantage of Joram's turmoil to urge repeatedly that Jezebel be exiled. Each time, Joram refused. But it always meant an argument. And it always ended with Joram stomping out in anger.

"Perhaps it's better the way it is," Obadiah suggested after the most recent confrontation. "At least this way we know where Jezebel is. We know what she's doing, and what she can and cannot do. We have control of her."

"No one has control of Jezebel except the devil himself." Elisha laughed mirthlessly.

The old Master of the Royal Palaces shook his head, walked to a window, and looked out across the parched and listless city. "How much longer will this drouth and famine last?"

"The Lord said seven years."

Obadiah shook his head. "Only four have yet passed."

"The kingdom will not be healed until Jezebel is either exiled or dead."

"The people are in a bad way, Elisha. Many of them cannot last three months. Let alone another three years."

"Jezebel influences sin too much, I tell you, Obadiah."

"But not *all* the people are influenced by Jezebel. They're not *all* bad. How can the Lord, in all his mercy and wisdom, ask such a trial of the good and the bad together?"

Elisha made no answer.

Obadiah gave a heavy sigh, turned, and walked back toward him with a weary smile. "It is as I have long suspected. The reasons for God's doings are often hidden. Even from his own holy men!"

Elisha rubbed at his bald head and said nothing.

The door to the chamber swung open. Joram strode in and stopped just inside while the two palace guards with him waited outside the door. There was a strange tension about him. He looked as if he had been drinking. Yet scarcely an hour before, when they had all been together, he had been stone-cold sober. He held a small, rolled-up parchment in one hand and stood looking first at Obadiah, then at Elisha.

Obadiah went to him. "How can I help you, sire?"

A strained expression showed in Joram's eyes. "I have learned two pieces of news within the past few minutes which disturb me greatly." He handed the parchment to Obadiah, crossed to a chair, and sat down.

Obadiah unrolled the parchment, read it through, and glanced at Elisha. "King Jehoram of Judah is dead."

"Dead? How?"

"Struck down by the same feverish illness that has plagued him for some time, according to this message."

"I should go to his funeral," Elisha said, half to himself. "Just out of the respect I had for his late father, King Jehoshaphat."

"What about respect for my sister and her son, Ahaziah, who is now King of Judah? Don't they deserve some of your holy approval?"

"I wonder what kind of ruler he will make."

"You'll know soon enough. Jehoram's funeral will be within a few days. Sometime after that Ahaziah's coronation will take place. Then you can see what kind of ruler he will be, Prophet!"

Elisha ignored him.

"Besides, Prophet, that's a peculiar question for you to ask when you're the man with all the foreknowledge and predictions . . . and the power of resurrection."

Again Elisha ignored him.

"Will you want to leave at once for Jerusalem, sire?" Obadiah asked, not wanting another argument to start.

"I don't know. There are problems to be solved first."

"Problems?"

"My mother, for one thing."

"Yes, of course. She'll want to go because of Athaliah."

"But I don't want to take her," Joram declared. "There will be security problems, baggage problems, and arguments. Ceaseless arguments. It isn't worth it. Besides, it breaks her imprisonment, and I don't want to do that."

"She disliked Jehoram so much, perhaps she'd prefer going just to the coronation. I could take her, if you like," Obadiah offered.

"She won't go with you. She thinks you're loyal to me."

"Perhaps we should tell her she can't go for reasons of her own safety," Obadiah suggested as an alternative.

Joram went to a chair and sat down. "Or better yet, why don't we keep the news from her until we're ready for her to know?"

Joram's words and facial expression signaled trouble. He seemed no longer to be talking about Jezebel. Elisha glanced at Obadiah. The old man had stiffened as if readying himself for defense.

"Not tell?" Elisha asked.

"Isn't that your advice? To keep silent until it suits one's own convenience? Isn't that it, Prophet?"

"Why not? Considering the problems otherwise created," Elisha said in a practical tone, still uncertain of Joram's real meaning.

"Isn't that the same advice you've been giving to Obadiah and Benaiah in recent times?"

The question came like an arrow from ambush.

Obadiah frowned.

"Isn't that the same advice you've been giving to Obadiah and Benaiah?" Joram repeated, mistrust and open dislike in his accusing look.

"Advice? About what?"

"About the absence of Merari and Nahum from Shunem!"

He glanced toward Obadiah and bluffed, "What's he talking about?"

"He's talking about the Shunammites' trip to Philistia, Elisha. And about their extended visit with Merari's relatives."

"Extended visit? Rot! They've moved away!" Joram got to his feet. An angry flush darkened his face. He came toward them with such vehemence that Elisha took a step backward. It was the wrong thing to do. Joram pressed the advantage, singling him out as the real target. "Isn't it enough that you stir up constant unrest among my people with your talk of your Jehovah? Isn't it enough that you nag at me to exile my own mother? And now—now I find that you have lied to me."

Elisha stopped dead in his tracks. "How have I lied to you?"

"You have deceived me about my beloved."

"Your beloved?"

"Sire!" Obadiah admonished. "Merari is not your beloved. She's a married woman. She's—"

"And you." Joram wheeled on the old man. "You who are supposed to be loyal to me. You, too, have deceived me. You've made a fool of me! For how long, old man? A month? A year? Four years?"

Elisha intervened. "How have we made a fool of you, Joram?"

Joram shrugged him off.

"We've never lied to you," Obadiah protested.

"You never told me they were gone!"

"You never asked, sire."

Joram swore and motioned for the guards to come in. "Arrest the prophet!"

"But, sire, the prophet is your friend, as I am your friend," Obadiah protested.

"He is no friend. He moved Merari out of the kingdom. Out of my reach. He is banished—from my palace and my city!"

"Sire, I protest."

"Throw him out!" Joram ordered the guards. "And throw out his loose-tongued servant, Gehazi, as well."

Elisha put up no struggle. Even before the guards reached him, he was moving toward the doorway. Neither guard touched him. They simply escorted him carefully away from the irate Joram.

Eyes wild, Joram turned on Obadiah. "Never again play me for the fool, old man. Never again!" He wheeled about, strode back through the doorway and down a wide corridor that led to the barracks of the chariot corps. "Jehu, Commander Jehu!" His shouts echoed eerily against the stone walls but brought no response. Twice more he shouted before an answer came—not from Jehu, but from Gershom, a captain of the chariot corps from Ibleam.

"Where is Commander Jehu?"

"In the city, sire."

"Where in the city?"

"I'm not sure where."

"Then, you'll have to do. Bring me seven pair of my sandals. Ready two chariots for travel. Meet me at the west gate as fast as possible. We're going to Shunem."

Sunset, crimson and gold, teased the landscape by the time they reached the most southerly parcel of land privately owned by Nahum and Obadiah. Joram, followed by an unquestioning but curious Captain Gershom, pulled his horses to a stop and breathed deeply for the first time since they left Samaria. He handed the reins to the captain and climbed down from the chariot.

"Hand me one pair of my sandals, Captain."

The charioteer did as he was ordered.

Joram took them and looked around for the property marker. Almost immediately, he saw it a few yards away. A pile of stones, dug from the very field they identified, were set up in a triangular shape. The top stone was carved with the emblems of Obadiah and Nahum. Joram walked to it, and with great ceremonious care laid his sandals next to its base on the land it marked. He straightened up and stood looking at it in satisfaction. Three more parcels of land owned by Nahum and Obadiah would be similarly reclaimed, as well as three parcels belonging to Benaiah, Zibia, and Merari. All of them, except for two that had been handed down by Zibia's Philistine ancestors, had been given originally as reward for loyal service. Now they were being reclaimed in retribution for loyal service violated. Once done, the whole expanse of this portion of the great Plain of Jezreel would belong to the royal court of Israel once again.

"Captain Gershom, you are my witness. I have placed my sandals on this soil. The land is now mine. The owners are absent. My sandals now signify my claim and my possession."

In customary fashion, the captain gave a formal salute. "I so witness your possession of this land, sire."

Joram returned to his chariot and boarded. Gershom handed him the reins and followed him in a westerly direction to complete the act of vengeance.

By the time the seventh and last section of land had been repossessed, and they had turned their chariots back toward Samaria, Joram's penchant for secrecy had overtaken his sense of satisfaction. He reminded himself that he really knew nothing about this captain from Ibleam whom he had pressed into service. The fact that he held the rank of captain meant only that he was a qualified charioteer; it gave no clue to his ability to keep silent about the night's events. Suppose he had a loose-tongue like Elisha's servant. What then? Suppose he should mention this night's activities to Obadiah.

Benaiah and Obadiah were still important and useful. Yet if they learned of his acts this night, they would surely abandon him. And that would be unfortunate.

- 15 -

A contrite and spirit-burdened Gehazi caught up with Elisha at a favorite campsite on the road leading northeastward from Samaria to Beth-shan. Joram's palace guards had not treated him with the same respect they had shown to the prophet. Blood from a head wound had trickled down onto his forehead and dried there. The skin around one eye was swollen and purple. His cloak, which Tamar had fashioned for him from sheepskins, had a jagged tear in it from a knife-thrust. His appearance made it obvious that the guards had had rough sport with him before turning him loose.

In spite of the fact that Gehazi had probably provoked the rough treatment with his wagging tongue, Elisha felt sorry for him. Gehazi seemed to have more imperfections than most men; and he seemed to learn less from his experiences than most. Sometimes Elisha wondered why he bothered to keep him as his servant. Since he had married Tamar, Gehazi was even more slack in his work. He complained more loudly than ever when travel was required. Tamar spoiled him, catered to him, was not offended by his boastfulness.

"You talk too much, Gehazi. I've told you that before."

"I swear to you, my master, it wasn't my intent to tell anything that—" he professed as Elisha tended his head wound.

"And I've warned you about it. This time, Nahum and Merari may be endangered by your loose talk."

"Yes, master, but I—ouch!"

"And you're boastful, Gehazi. Much too boastful. God's

men are not supposed to take the credit for His acts."

"Yes, master. But the guards said—"

"And you've turned lazy and self-centered. That's the worst of all." Elisha stood up and handed Gehazi the rag he had moistened in the shallow brook that seeped half-hidden through the stand of acacias. "I've cleaned your head wound. It isn't deep. Keep the rag on it a moment. The bleeding has almost stopped."

"Thank you."

Elisha went back to the small campfire where two young quail were roasting.

"Fresh meat?" Gehazi's one good eye bulged in delight.

"I suppose you're hungry, too."

Gehazi gave a crooked smile. "I can always eat, master."

"Then here, you tend these birds. Turn them often and don't let them burn. Call me when they're ready." He handed over the small willow branch he'd been using to turn the quail. "And Gehazi."

"Yes, master?"

"Don't talk to me."

A subdued look swept over the servant's face.

"I wish to meditate." He moved a short distance away, sat down, leaned back against a small boulder and closed his eyes. The moment he did so, the vision which so recently had begun to recur occupied his mind once more. For the past several days, every time he closed his eyes—and sometimes even in quiet moments when he didn't—he could see himself crossing the Jordan River at the fording place near Beth-shan. Then, in a disconnected sequence, he would see himself going north toward Damascus, where King Ben-Hadad lay ill. But he never saw himself going into the city. Instead, all he could see was one of the king's commanders in earnest conversation with him. The man's face wasn't known to him, but every feature was clearly visible. And his own actions puzzled him: he was acting as if he was preparing the man for some great task, even though he didn't know who he was. The vision—dreamlike and disconnected as it was—had become so persistent, and so vivid, that he knew it was another way the Lord was speaking to him. Because of that certainty, he had actually started the journey toward Damascus.

Impulse had caused his fateful detour to Samaria. He had learned that Joram had returned there from battle for a short rest. He wanted to talk with him once again in the hope of persuading him to exile Jezebel. Riddance of her from the kingdom would shorten the drouth and its resulting famine. But now he regretted having followed his impulse. His efforts with Joram had failed. In fact, the stop in Samaria might have done more harm than he yet knew. He should have made his journey straight to Beth-shan and beyond to Damascus. That's what the Lord had told him to do. He should have obeyed.

He felt a tap at his shoulder and opened his eyes. Darkness had come. The small campfire was burning low and Gehazi leaned near him holding out the cooked quail.

They ate in silence, then checked on the horses tethered nearby and bedded down under the star-spattered blackness of the night until the first pale gray of sunrise roused them and sent them on their journey.

Early in the forenoon of the second day a caravan, amidst its own great cloud of dust, approached from the north. As the intervening distance diminished, Elisha counted forty camels. Each was heavily laden. Moving in a majestic, rhythmic gait, they were before him in a very short time and pulling to a halt.

He reined in his horse. Gehazi did likewise.

The man on the lead camel looked at him carefully, appraising his face and his bald head. "You are the prophet Elisha?"

"I am."

The man slid down from his camel, handed the reins to a drover, came forward and made a low, full salaam to Elisha. When he straightened, he pulled back his tarbush, fully revealing his face.

A tremor went through Elisha. It was the man in his vision: the same square face with its combative expression, the eyebrows that made a straight line above the eyes, and the thin, straight lips that curled into a natural sneer when he smiled.

"I am Hazael, aide to King Ben-Hadad of Damascus, who lies ill in that city."

Elisha waited.

"My king has sent me forth to meet you, and to present you with gifts." He gestured toward the forty camels. "Every good thing of Damascus is in those bales."

"Why bring me gifts?"

"Because my king has need of your knowledge."

"What knowledge might that be?"

"My king asks if he will recover from his sickness."

With a sense of foreboding, Elisha studied the man's face. The whispering voice he knew so well began speaking to his spirit, urging him to give the Lord's message to Hazael.

"Well, m'lord?"

Elisha glanced away, listening for yet another moment to the whispering voice.

"Well, m'lord?" Hazael insisted. "Will my king, Ben-Hadad, recover from his sickness?"

Elisha nodded. "Go and say to him that he shall surely recover from his illness."

A cold expression had come into Hazael's eyes; it did not waver.

"But also say to him that the Lord has shown me that he will really die!"

The thin, straight lips curled into the narrowest of smiles.

The whispering voice in Elisha's spirit continued, revealing all that was to come in the future. A great siege. Cannibalism. Death. Danger. Sadness. For uncounted moments, he stared at Hazael's unforgiving countenance. It was a symbol, he thought. A symbol of Israel's future. Without repentance, Israel's future and that of Hazael were linked

together. A great sadness welled up inside him. So great
was it that tears filled his eyes.

"Why do you cry, man of God?" Hazael's tone was con-
temptuous. "Ben-Hadad is no friend of yours. Nor of your
country."

"My tears are for you."

"Me? Why me?"

"Because I know the evil you will do to the children of
Israel."

"What evil?"

"You will set their strongholds on fire. You will kill their
young men with swords. You will dash their children, and
rip open the women with child."

"What am I? A dog? Why should I do such evil things?"

"Oh, you will do them, Hazael. You will try to destroy
all Israel. And you will try very soon. For the Lord has
shown me that you will become king in Ben-Hadad's
place."

Hazael stepped back in astonishment. Quickly he glanced
about to see who might have overheard the prophetic
words. But only Gehazi was near enough to have heard;
and his face was turned away in apparent disinterest.

A calculating expression hardened the astonished look in
Hazael's face. He turned again to Elisha. "The gifts from
Ben-Hadad still are yours, Prophet. And, if what you say is
true, they are from me, also."

Elisha bowed as if Hazael's unwarranted generosity did
not surprise him. "Will your drovers take them on to Samaria for me?"

Hazael turned, shouted orders in a strange dialect to the
lead drover, and in almost immediate response the caravan
moved forward once again toward the Kingdom of Israel.
As the last of the camels went by, Hazael returned to his
own camel, remounted, and with a final salute headed back
north toward Damascus.

Elisha watched him go. "Famine and drouth. Disease and

destruction. It is happening. All of it. The word of the Lord is right. The word of the Lord is true."

"Master, look!" Gehazi pointed south in the direction taken by the caravan. It was hidden from view by this time. But the great cloud of dust kicked up by the camels was visible in the glassy sky; and it had a curious kink in it, as if somewhere, beyond the far ridge, the caravan had changed direction and was moving away from the borders of Israel in a great circle that would take it north toward Damascus!

Elisha gave a mirthless laugh.

"But, master," Gehazi protested, "they're stealing your goods! We must do something!"

"Do what? There are two of us. There are at least half a hundred of them. Besides—the goods were never really mine, Gehazi."

The servant looked puzzled and very disapproving.

"Those goods belonged to Ben-Hadad in the first place. Now, it seems, they will belong to his successor. It's just as well. We won't be back in Samaria for quite a long time. Joram banished us. Or had you so soon forgotten?"

Gehazi blushed.

Elisha turned his horse and set off in a southwesterly direction.

"Where are we going now?" Gehazi yelled.

"Jerusalem."

"Jerusalem?"

"King Jehoram of Judah is dead. I'm surprised you hadn't heard. I learned of it in Samaria. Just before we were banished." He kicked his horse into a trot, with a bewildered Gehazi trailing behind.

Three days later, after pressing hard in order not to be late for the ceremonies, they crested a final ridge and saw before them the walls of the city of Jerusalem. Rising from the prominence of Mount Moriah, the great Temple dazzled in the morning sunlight like a precious jewel. Streaming out from the walls in every direction were hundreds and thousands of travelers. Like banners fluttering in a gentle breeze, the long lines of people swayed and undulated according to the winding of the roads. But all moved toward the great city. On the hills surrounding the outskirts of Jerusalem were the tents and temporary encampments most of them had brought with them.

"Did all these people come for the funeral?" Gehazi asked.

Elisha didn't hear him. He had moved forward into a band of wayfarers, and not until they reached the Kidron Valley did Gehazi catch up with him again.

They passed through the valley at the base of the great limestone walls surrounding the Temple Mount, until they came to the gate called Zion. Inside was that portion of Jerusalem that King David had built; and beyond, to the northwest, rose the walls of the palace built by Solomon. Every king since had added to the palace. It was very large. Cavernous. Dark and dank. And yet, in many ways, it matched the wonders of Egypt and of Babylon. Its gardens and courtyards were alive with color. Oleander, hibiscus, and bougainvilla flourished amid palms and cypress trees. Its rooms of state were furnished with the masterful works of carpenters and cabinet makers, weavers and potters. And the private chambers boasted even greater comfort and beauty, Elisha reminded himself as they drew up to a side entrance and dismounted.

Leaving Gehazi to tend the horses, he hurried through an open courtyard and slipped into the west gallery of the palace. Though he had not been here since before Jehoshaphat's death, he remembered well the avenues of entrance and exit. In these days, he wondered idly, whether they should be called avenues of entrance and escape? Jehoram had never taken to the idea of his father welcoming Jehovah's prophets and having them as guests for months at a time so that he could talk religion with them and share his faith. Now that Jehoram, too, was dead, Elisha wondered if he had passed his distaste for Jehovah's prophets on to his son Ahaziah, the new king. It would not be unlikely. Especially considering the fact that the boy's mother was the daughter of Jezebel and sister to Joram of Israel!

He turned from the west gallery and slowed to a stop. The funeral ceremony was in progress in the great colonnaded audience hall, which was packed with people. From the far end came the chanting of funeral rituals, somber, mournful. He moved quietly to one side, pulled the hood of his mantle up over his head, and folded his hands together. There, full in the midst of those mourning a weak, evil, and unbelieving man, Elisha, the prophet, spoke his own silent prayers to Jehovah, asking the one true God to forgive *all* men of their sins; praising the Holy Name of Jehovah and thanking him for all the good wrought for humankind; and fervently asking for the surcease of the drouth and the famine, disease, and destruction that ravaged good and bad alike in the land of Israel. So deeply did he meditate in his prayer that only when a hand touched his arm did he once again become aware of where he was. He turned to find Nahum standing at his side. Delighted, he grabbed Nahum's forearm and clung to it in customary greeting.

A cortege of high-ranking men of the royal court of Judah moved past them, carrying the bier of Jehoram the King out to its place of burial alongside his father, Jehoshaphat.

"Merari? Is she here, too?" he whispered.

Nahum nodded in the direction of the recession which followed the royal bier out of the audience hall. "She's with Athaliah. And so is our son."

"Ozem? Here?" He felt more eager to see the boy than he had ever imagined. He had missed these friends since they had moved to Joppa. Until this instant, he hadn't realized how much.

"You won't recognize Ozem." Nahum's pride in the boy showed in his eyes. "Nor will you recognize Hakkatan."

"Jehu's orphan?"

"He's like our second son, Elisha."

The prophet studied his old friend with renewed respect and remembered again the hospitality of this kindly man and his wife. Of all the people he knew, he felt closest to them, and cared the most about them.

"Both boys are practically grown—or at least they think they are! They're eleven and twelve now. And I think they'll be fine men one day."

At that moment, Elisha caught sight of Merari walking close behind Athaliah. She was looking straight ahead, her face expressionless. Beside her, and almost as tall as she, walked a serious-faced young lad.

"Ozem?" Elisha whispered.

"Yes. And Hakkatan is just behind him, walking with Zibia."

He noted with surprise that both boys looked enough alike to have been blood brothers. The exception was their coloring. Ozem, favored his mother. He was blonde, fair-skinned and with eyes the color of aquamarine. Hakkatan, on the other hand, was black-haired, olive-skinned and had dark eyes.

"Where are you staying, Elisha?" Nahum asked as they fell into step and followed the recession out of the great colonnaded hall into the morning sunlight.

"I'm not sure. Gehazi and I have just arrived. And I'm not at all certain of the reception I'll be accorded by Judah's new king. By the way," he interrupted himself, "did Joram come for the ceremonies?"

Nahum shook his head. "He sent Benaiah in his place. Since Merari is a friend of Athaliah, Benaiah thought whole family should come, too. Now that you're here, I'm glad we came. I hope we'll all have a chance for a good visit, Elisha."

"We must *make* the chance. There's much news to share."

"We leave for Joppa tomorrow." Nahum said. "Can you come with us? A rest might do you good."

The idea delighted him. It would be good to rest for a

while, especially in the company of such good friends. "Let me pray about it, Nahum. I'll get word to you before darkness descends this day."

"Good. We're staying here in the palace. Just off the west gallery."

"Until later then." Elisha set off to find Gehazi and the horses. By the time he reached them, he'd made up his mind to go to Joppa.

"Gehazi," he said quietly, coming up behind the dozing servant.

Startled, Gehazi jumped up quickly.

"How would you like to go back to Shunem today?"

"You mean it, sir?"

"I mean it. In fact, you can leave immediately if you wish."

"But . . . but, I don't understand."

"You need the rest, Gehazi. And I do, too."

The servant grinned. "You always rest well in Shunem."

"I'm not going to Shunem. I've been invited to return to Joppa with Nahum and Merari."

"Nahum is here?"

Elisha nodded.

"With his family?"

Elisha nodded again.

"And you're going with them to Joppa?"

"I think so. If the Lord wants me to, I will."

The servant glanced around in an agitated fashion, as if he'd lost something.

"What's wrong, Gehazi?"

"I don't want to go to Joppa. I want to go to Shunem. To Tamar."

"Then go!"

"You mean it, master?"

Elisha laughed. "Of course I mean it. Go!"

"Oh yes, master." He mounted his horse. "And I know Tamar will be glad to see me."

Elisha waved him off and set out for the Temple Mount

where he prayed and meditated until the shadows of a vanishing day spread deeply across the Temple enclosure. Then he returned to the palace to find Nahum and tell him of his decision to go with them to Joppa.

The journey itself took only a day. It was short enough not to be tiring, and long enough for good trail talk. Merari chose to ride on horseback with him and Nahum and the two boys, rather than in the carryalls with Zibia and Aunt Ilia; and so the three of them were able to exchange bits of news and bring each other up-to-date on happenings of the last four years. He told them about the severity of the encroaching drouth; about Tamar and Gehazi and their happiness in marriage. And he told them about his most recent confrontation with Joram and about Joram's reaction when he finally learned of their move to Joppa. "He went into a rage bordering on madness," he said. "Joram is still in love with you, Merari."

She blushed and glanced at Nahum for reassurance.

"We know that he is still in love with her," confirmed Nahum. "It's sad in a way, because she doesn't love him."

They went on to tell him of their quiet life in Joppa. They enjoyed the sights and sounds of the seacoast city. But they had not completely lost touch with the land. Nahum recently had established a small farming operation in the Plain of Philistia, on a parcel of land that Aunt Ilia's husband had left to her. Mainly, though, they spoke about the two boys and the joy of raising them.

"Jehu has come several times to see Hakkatan," Nahum said.

"That surprises me, considering how jealous Joram is of his commander's time."

Merari laughed. "Jehu is very clever with disguises."

"Hakkatan is devoted to him," Nahum offered. "He talks about him all the time."

"Almost as much as Ozem talks about you, Elisha."

It was good trail talk, satisfying for them all. Elisha found himself laughing more than he had in a long time. One of the nicest things about his friendship with Merari and Nahum, he realized, was that no matter how long the separation, reunion with them was without strain, and the conversation was spontaneous. It was a pleasurable relationship, far removed from the strife and violence and sadness that seemed to be everywhere in the Kingdom of Israel. He offered a prayer of thanksgiving for the friendship, and for this opportunity to enjoy it.

For several weeks, he tarried in Joppa. He rested, meditated, went to the new farm with Nahum, walked along the seashore with Merari, and instructed the boys in the Law of Moses, the words of David and Solomon, and the ways of the Lord. Both boys were full of curiosity about his life as a prophet, and they were very attentive to his words. Hakkatan appeared to have a reverence for the land and farming. He often excused himself to go with Nahum to the new farm. But Ozem clearly showed the signs of Merari's influence. His interest in things pertaining to the Lord was surprising, unless one knew of the miraculous circumstance that allowed him still to be alive.

"Was I really dead, as my mother tells me? Or was I simply in a deep sleep, as our Aunt Ilia describes it?" he asked one day.

"How did your spirit feel?" Elisha countered. "Or were you too young to remember?"

The boy thought for a moment. "It felt as though I was slipping, I think."

"Slipping?"

The boy nodded. A frown of concentration made him seem older than his eleven years. "Yes, like I was slipping away toward a great darkness. But something kept hanging onto me. Something kept me from slipping too far toward the darkness. It was like . . ." He glanced out toward the Great Sea which stretched beyond the harbor at the foot of the hill where they were seated. "It was like you feel when you're swimming, or floating."

"Suspended?"

Ozem's frown lightened. "That's it! Suspended. The darkness was on one side. A light was on the other. I was just there. Between them."

Silence settled easily around them for a time. A breeze, playful and unpredictable, brought sounds from the harbor and the smell of salt air up to them.

"My mother says you resurrected me," Ozem finally said in a quiet tone, looking up at him.

He turned and searched the boy's eyes. They were clear, unafraid, eager for knowledge. "It was the Lord who resurrected you, my son. Not I. Such power resides only in the Lord. He only used me as his instrument. But it was your mother's unswerving faith that called the power of the Lord into action. She never gave up, Ozem. She never claimed your death by her words. In fact, she rejected the mere idea of it. You were such a special gift from the Lord to your parents that she simply refused to allow the darkness to take you."

The boy sat very still, staring across the distance to the Great Sea. "Then it is as she says: I really do belong to the Lord, don't I?"

"Yes, my son, you do. All of us who believe belong to him, if we would but know it."

The boy pulled his knees up, folded his arms over them, rested his chin on his arms, and stared out to the sea.

Elisha got to his feet and stretched. "I promised your mother we'd be back by the noonday hour. We'd best go." He reached down and helped the boy up.

As they began walking back to the house, Merari came hurrying toward them, waving and motioning for them to come quickly.

They hurried after her. As they rounded the corner of the wall and went through the gate into the courtyard, Gehazi, who had just arrived from Shunem, came rushing toward them.

"Master! Samaria! It's besieged!"

"Besieged? By whom?"

"Ben-Hadad and all his army. At least at first. Now it's besieged by Hazael." Fear was in the servant's face. "Ben-Hadad is dead. As you prophesied, Hazael is now King of Damascus. He continues to besiege Samaria."

Elisha put his hand on the man's shoulder. "Be calm, Gehazi. Tell me slowly of this terrible thing. When did the siege begin?"

"While we were in Jerusalem, I think, m'lord."

"But that was weeks ago."

"Yes, m'lord, and it has been going on ever since. And the hunger! Oh, master, famine is full upon those in Samaria."

The entire household of Aunt Ilia was now in the courtyard, gathering close to hear Gehazi's report.

"The famine is so great," he went on in a shaky voice, "that a donkey's head was sold for eighty shekels of silver. Dove droppings are selling for five shekels."

Aunt Ilia turned away, sickened at the mere report.

"How did you learn this?" Nahum asked.

"From your uncle, sir."

"Obadiah?"

Gehazi nodded. "He came to Shunem just yesterday to give us the report." He turned to Elisha again. "And he sent me here to warn you, my master."

Zibia pressed forward. "What about my husband, the Honorable Benaiah?"

"He's not in Samaria, ma'am. He's still in Phoenicia, seeking an army to help break the siege."

"What about Jehu?" Merari asked, her eyes wide with concern.

"He's with the king, m'lady."

"Where is Joram?" Elisha asked. "Did he flee to Jezreel?"

"No. He's still in Samaria. Each night he walks the top of the walls, surveying the Syrians in their camp. But two nights ago—" Gehazi stopped and swallowed hard.

"What about two nights ago?"

"Two nights ago, the king learned that a woman, driven mad by hunger, had boiled and eaten her own son!"

Shock and revulsion paralyzed them all. Unable and unwilling to accept such grossness, each person present stared in stupefaction at the servant of the prophet.

Elisha recalled the warning that had come to him in the vision: Drouth and famine. Siege. Cannibalism. Death. Sorrow throughout the land.

"King Joram tore his clothes when he heard this report. Now he wears sackcloth. He thinks that you, master, are the cause of the siege and the famine. He blames you. And he blames the Lord God Jehovah. He has sent men to find you and cut off your head, master. That's what the Honorable Obadiah sent me to warn you about."

Concern showing plainly on their faces, Merari and Nahum came to Elisha. "You must stay on here in Joppa. He cannot touch you here."

Elisha choked back a sudden feeling of nausea, forced a smile onto his face, and acknowledged their kindness.

"They're right, master. You should stay somewhere out of Israel."

"What of Jezebel?" Elisha asked. "Has Joram rid the land of her?"

"Aye, master. That he has. He has sent her to Jerusalem for her grandson's coronation, and there she's to stay."

"If Athaliah will let her," Zibia put in.

"Has the siege spread beyond the city of Samaria?" Nahum asked.

"No sir. Only the city itself is besieged."

Elisha turned and walked to the far side of the courtyard. Merari followed him.

"I must go back," he murmured to himself.

She overheard. "Why? To let Joram cut off your head and make a martyr of you?"

"To help break the siege on Samaria. I've met Hazael. Perhaps I can persuade him to break the siege."

"But you told us that the siege was in your vision,"

Merari reminded him. "That it's the will of the Lord."

"Yes, but that defilement, Jezebel, is now out of the country. That will make a difference."

"But what if it doesn't make a difference? What if you're caught by Joram's men and beheaded?"

"Then the siege will continue. Thousands more will die, and—"

"And Israel will have no spiritual leader, because you will be dead!" Merari pressed.

"But, Merari," he protested.

"Merari is right," Nahum cut in, joining them. "It is suicide for you to return. And useless suicide at that, unless you can break the siege."

Elisha looked at them, knowing they were right, weighing their words again, uncertain about what he should do. The other members of the household were crowding in close to hear their conversation. He rubbed at his beard, wishing for privacy to think this through.

"We need to let Elisha think before he makes a decision," Merari said, glancing at the rest of the household. They turned away, understanding the prophet's need.

"Let us help you, Elisha," Nahum said. "Come, Merari and I will find a place where we can talk this out."

- 16 -

The quiet place Nahum and Merari found was the open hillside overlooking Joppa's harbor near the spot where Elisha and Ozem had been earlier. A single, ancient oak sentineled this part of the hillside. They sat down beside its sturdy trunk, in the leafy canopy of shade.

"There is a way to break the siege, Elisha," Nahum offered.

"What way?"

"The wheat and barley in the storehouses at Shunem."

It took a moment before Elisha realized the impact of Nahum's offer.

"In fact," Nahum went on, "there is enough grain stored in Shunem from the royal lands alone to feed several cities the size of Samaria. Not to mention the harvests from our family-owned lands."

"Joram probably doesn't know it's there. Obadiah tells me that he pays little attention to the grain reports."

"And you're willing to offer it to him?"

Nahum nodded in agreement.

Elisha looked at his old friend in dismay. "You would do this to help Joram?"

"No. But I would help starving people. I would help rout a foe. I may not like Joram, Elisha, but I love my country."

"I don't know," Elisha objected. "How would we get that much grain inside the city's walls without being seen by the enemy?"

"Those things can be worked out. Those are details."

A sudden breeze, refreshed with the smell of the sea, set the oak leaves above them to dancing and caused dapples of sunlight to play tag with each other on the ground.

Elisha turned to Merari. "What do you think?"

"I think Nahum is right. Those are mere details. They can be worked out." She smiled. "But I think there's another, more important point to discuss."

"What point is that?"

"We can use the grain to get Joram to take back his order that you are to be captured and beheaded."

Both men looked at her in astonishment.

That thought obviously had not occurred to either of them. How like men to focus on the action of warfare, rather than on their own danger. She plucked at a blade of grass and waited. As far as she was concerned, protecting Elisha was the most important point of all. God's holy prophet must not die at the hands of riffraff because of Joram! "Lifting the death edict and protecting God's holy prophet of Israel is far more important than lifting the siege of Samaria," she said quietly.

"But how—?" Elisha exclaimed.

"By using the grain to bargain with. Joram calls off your death edict, and we give him grain for his besieged city."

"He'll never agree to that. His hate for me is too great."

"He might do it for another reason," Nahum said calmly. "He might do it for Merari!"

Elisha stared. First at Nahum, who in turn was watching intently for a reaction from Merari.

To her own surprise, she returned their questioning looks directly, without blushing and with no sense of shame or guilt. In fact, the more she thought about it, the more her sense of exhilaration grew. What righteous retribution it would be to bargain directly, face-to-face, with Joram and defeat him in order to protect their friend Elisha! Sounds drifted up from the harbor and were carried away as rapidly by another sudden breeze.

"It would be dangerous," the prophet said softly.

"You're worth the risk, old friend. All will be well."

At first light the next morning, they bid farewell to the

rest of the family and set out on horseback for Shunem. Kallai and Gehazi rode with them. They rode hard, and by the fall of night arrived at the compound.

Their return to Shunem was greeted with a joyousness that made their hearts sing. Uncle Obadiah rushed forward and gave them each a hug so strong that it belied the signs of age and stress showing in his face. Tamar, they discovered, was beginning to grow large with child. "Now *that,* Gehazi, is something you should be talking about," Elisha teased.

By the following morning, the whole village knew of their return and had come to the compound to greet them. Nahum and Merari took the occasion to explain the reason for their return and asked for help from everyone to prepare a caravan of grain carts that could be taken to Samaria. Nahum instructed the field foremen to recheck all the fields for any grains that might have been left over from the last harvest.

"What about the marker corners, sir? Shall we cut them, too?" The question came from the young foreman who had the job of managing the family-owned lands. "We've never fully cut those seven parcels, but as you instructed have let hedgerows grow as shelter for the birds and wildlife."

"Cut them now. There may be more there than we realize."

By midday, the foreman returned looking for Nahum. He found him in the pottery shed with Merari. "The marker corners, sir—there *is* more there than we knew!"

The man's excitement was obvious.

"What do you mean?" Nahum asked.

"I mean, sir, that we've found the king's sandals placed on the land beside your ownership marker!"

"The king's sandals?" Merari asked, astonished. "How do you know they're his?"

"The leather thongs are branded with his royal signet. And the sandals look as if they've been there for several weeks. And . . . they're all alike!"

"All alike?"

"Yes, sir. There are seven pairs of sandals. One pair on each piece of property owned by you and your uncle and by Benaiah's family."

Nahum's face paled with anger.

"Wait outside," Merari ordered the foreman. Then, fighting down her own anger, she went to Nahum. "It doesn't matter. We've found him out. He cannot confiscate our lands. There are laws. The land is still ours."

"I should have killed him years ago."

"Don't say that."

"I *should* have killed him!" he repeated, walking away. "I had the chance years ago. You should never have stopped me."

"Shouldn't I?"

"No, you shouldn't have!" he stormed.

For a long moment, she watched him pace back and forth, venting his anger in muttered oaths, his fists clenching and unclenching and clenching again. Only once before had she seen him so enraged: when he stopped Joram from raping her. Now she could almost see his mind at work. First his woman, and now his land. Joram had attempted to violate them both. Nahum had retaliated by marrying his woman. But as for the retaliation for his land . . . She moved toward him, knowing that she could let him exercise his rage no further. "Then perhaps we should never have married, either!"

He stopped short and turned to stare at her.

"If you had killed Joram that day years ago, someone would have been sent to kill you. We would never have married then. If you kill Joram now, again someone will be sent to kill you. Only now, if that happens, you'll give Joram the victory after all."

A puzzled look overrode the anger in his face.

"Yes, my husband. A victory. For Joram. Through Jezebel," she went on. "For if you kill Joram now, Jezebel will have you killed. And you will leave a widow and a son who hasn't yet reached manhood as her prey and as her victims!"

"Merari is right, my nephew," Obadiah said from the open doorway behind them.

They both turned, startled.

Obadiah, with Elisha following, came into the pottery shed and closed the wooden door. "You're right to be angry about what Joram has done. But it isn't unexpected. That's why we all took such care to keep your move to Philistia such a secret."

"It's equally obvious," Elisha added, "that his attempted confiscation of your lands is only that. An attempt."

"So, my nephew, that makes Merari right, you see. Your best retaliation is not to kill Joram."

"What is it, then?" Nahum demanded.

"Follow the plan that brought you back here in the first place."

"Follow the plan? You mean—?"

"Sit down, my nephew. Sit down, Merari." He motioned them to a rough wooden bench and waited for them to do as he asked. Then he pulled up another bench and sat down directly in front of them.

Elisha moved to stand beside Nahum.

"Your plan to use Shunem's grains to bargain for the removal of the death edict for Elisha is a splendid one. Joram wants desperately to break the power of Hazael's siege. I think you don't realize how desperate he is for that. There's no reason why you can't use the same grain to bargain for the return of your lands, is there?"

Nahum started to protest, but Elisha put a restraining hand on his shoulder. "Hear him out."

"Joram's placing his sandals on your lands has no meaning. That custom is only good when the rightful owners move away permanently and don't visit the property for a full season or more. That's not the case here. Joram knows that. Your house is still furnished and in use. Benaiah and I have been living here, off and on, ever since you went to Joppa. Your servants are still here caring for it. Your field hands and foremen are still being paid and are still working. You have returned four times each year to check on the harvests and general condition of the lands. You haven't abandoned your land. His claim on them is meaningless."

A deepening sense of relief went through Merari.

"The second point, my nephew, is this. If Joram had really intended to make good his claim, he would have had a witness make his mark on a property record in the archives at the palace. That will be easy to check. And easier to destroy by a vote of the elders, if such a record exists."

"So you see, Nahum," Elisha said, giving his shoulder a friendly shake, "Joram has won nothing yet. Nor will he."

Nahum sighed and glanced at Merari for forgiveness. She grasped his hand and gave it a reassuring squeeze.

He stood up, went and opened the door of the shed, and called for the young foreman. "Go back to the fields and bring King Joram's sandals here to me."

"All of them, sir?"

"All of them. All seven pairs."

Within another day, all the villagers and workers had removed the harvested wheat and barley from the storehouses in Shunem and loaded it on a caravan of carts for transport to a secret place close to Samaria. There it would be safe until the bargaining with Joram could be accomplished.

By the time they were ready to move forward toward the secret hiding place, however, the villagers had learned of the incident of Joram's sandals. The revelation caused an uproar. As free men and women, they deeply resented the attempted confiscation. Field hands, who were to unload the carts once the final destination was reached, jumped off and started to walk away. Drivers dropped their reins, refusing to start the trek. "Why should we help a king who steals from Nahum and Merari?" they asked. Not until Nahum and Merari rode into their angry midst and pleaded with them for silence did they settle down.

"You say you respect us?" Nahum called out.

A great shout affirmed it.

"Do you respect the Honorable Obadiah and Benaiah?"

A second shout of approval went up.

"Would you like to help all of us right the wrong done by King Joram?"

The affirmative response came in a third shout, which was louder and lasted longer than the previous two.

"Then listen, my friends. Hear our words."

They quieted.

"Merari and I, along with the Honorable Obadiah, plan to use this grain you have all worked so hard to help us load to bargain for the return of our lands."

"You shouldn't have to bargain," a woman yelled from one side of the crowd. "The land already belongs to you. You and Merari have worked hard for it."

A rumble of agreement issued forth.

Nahum held up his hands for quiet. "What you say is true. We shouldn't have to. But there's something else the grain can be used to bargain for."

"We know," called out one of the village elders. "It will break the siege of Samaria."

"But that will help Joram," objected one of the cart drivers.

"Why should we help Joram?" someone else shouted.

Merari moved her horse forward a bit and then stood straight up in the stirrups. With help from Nahum, she motioned for silence.

Again the crowd quieted.

"Important as our land is to all of us," she said, "and as sad as the famine in Samaria is, there's an even more important reason for using this grain as a bargaining tool. It can be used to save the life of the prophet Elisha."

A startled hush fell over the assembly. They stared, disbelief in their faces, from Merari to Nahum to Obadiah to Elisha and back to Merari. How could a powerful man of God be in danger of his life? How could this holy prophet who had restored life to Ozem be in jeopardy himself? And yet Merari had never lied to them.

"King Joram is angry with the prophet Elisha," she went on. "He has decreed that the prophet is to be captured and beheaded!"

A rumble of shocked disapproval passed through the crowd.

"You and I—all of us—can keep that from happening. The grain is our bargaining tool. We must move it to a safe hiding place close to Samaria until the proper time." She paused, searching the faces in the crowd—hoping that she had persuaded them, uncertain that she had. "Will you help us?"

There was the briefest hesitation; then a thunderous shout of agreement erupted, reverberated against Mount Moreh, and echoed across the Plain of Jezreel!

The grain caravan went forward. By evening of the next day, all the carts were safely in hiding; and Merari, Nahum, Obadiah, and Elisha set out to bargain with Joram.

Their arrival at the Ivory Palace in the besieged city could not have been more stealthy if they had been wanted criminals.

"Of course, we *are,*" Elisha said with a thin laugh. "At least I am. It's rather a new role for me."

"Keep quiet! We'll all be prized prisoners if Hazael's men discover us," Obadiah reminded them. "Follow me."

He led them through a labyrinth of tunnels cut under the city walls and under the outer walls of the palace itself to a trap door which opened behind the large fountain in the center of Joram's private courtyard. They climbed up through the trap door and gently closed it.

Merari shuddered, glad to be out of the tunnel blackness. Here, torches blazed from their stanchions on surrounding walls and at intervals down the length of the gallery which led to the king's private chambers. The place was deserted. Only the plish-plash of the fountain broke the tomblike silence.

"Now what?" Nahum asked, leaning close to his uncle.

Before Obadiah could answer, the sound of approaching footsteps came from the direction of the throne room. Reflexively, all four of them pressed back into the shadows behind the fountain and waited.

The footsteps grew louder. Soon erratic patterns of moving light could be seen against the far wall of the gallery. The next thing they saw was Joram, torch in hand and staggering slightly, moving toward his private chambers.

Merari's heart caught in her throat. He was dressed in sackcloth. Ashes had been poured over his head, leaving his thick, dark hair gray and shaggy. His face was lined with stress, and deep circles gave his eyes a dull appearance.

He appeared to be alone. No further footsteps were heard. Mano-ah, his manservant, apparently had been dismissed for the night.

Motioning the others to stay hidden, Obadiah stepped from the shadows and salaamed. "Your Majesty . . ."

Joram jerked to a halt and turned. "Who's there?"

"It is I, Obadiah, sire."

Joram thrust forward the torch and peered at him. "Ah, yes, Obadiah. My trusted Master of the Royal Palaces. So you didn't desert me after all?"

"That depends, Your Majesty."

"On what? Hazael's determination to destroy my city? People have died. Did you know that, Obadiah?"

"Yes, sire."

"Hazael wanted to destroy me, too. He wanted this palace. Did you know that, Obadiah? This palace, built by my grandfather. That Syrian wanted it!"

"Yes, I know he does. But I may have found help for you."

"Help?"

"Yes, sire."

"What kind of help?"

"Foodstuffs. Grains, barley, wheat. With it, you can break Hazael's siege of this beleagured and dying city."

Joram's unsteadiness seemed to leave him. "Foodstuffs? To break the siege?"

"Yes, sire. On condition, of course."

"What condition?" he asked, suspiciously.

"There are two conditions, actually." Obadiah turned slightly and called out over his shoulder, "Come out now, if you will."

Nahum stepped out first, holding onto Merari with one hand and carrying a bulky sack in the other. Elisha followed closely after them.

The astonishment on Joram's face was matched only by his stunned silence.

As his silence lengthened, Obadiah took another step forward. "The conditions revolve around these people, sire. You can guess what those conditions are, I expect. But since time is of the essence, let me explain them to you clearly."

Joram tore his astonished stare away from Nahum, Merari, and Elisha to focus on Obadiah.

As if by rote, the old household minister stated the two conditions that would provide Joram with the grain from Shunem: rescind the death edict on Elisha, and admit publicly that the Shunem lands didn't belong to him.

Joram began slowly to nod his head. Whether the action indicated understanding of Obadiah's words, agreement to the conditions being stated, or total rejection of the proposal, none of them were quite sure. Joram suddenly stopped nodding his head and stood stock-still. He looked from one to the other of them, a strange new light glittering in his eyes. "You're too late, old man."

"Too late? In what way?"

"The Syrians have fled."

"Fled?" exclaimed Merari, Nahum, and Elisha in chorus.

Obadiah scowled. "Their camp is still outside the city walls."

"True. The tents and supplies are still there. But the Syrians themselves have fled. Jehu and his chariots are chasing them fast and far. I intend to join him quite soon." A sarcastic smile appeared on his face. "In fact, you're delaying me."

Elisha moved forward and blocked his way. "Why should the Syrians flee?" he asked, disbelieving. "What caused them to flee?"

"Nothing you had anything to do with, baldhead."

Elisha measured him with a penetrating look. "Jezebel is still in Jerusalem, isn't she? You rid the land of her, and now the siege has lifted. You finally did as I asked, didn't you?"

Joram's face darkened.

"Once more, you took the advice of Jehovah's prophet, didn't you?"

The strange glittering in Joram's eyes turned to pure malice. His hand slid to the hilt of the dagger at his waist. "Get out of my way, Prophet, or I will kill you myself, and behead you on the spot!"

"In front of your . . . 'beloved'?" Nahum accused.

The words stopped Joram. He snapped around to look at Merari.

In that moment, she loathed him, saw him for what he always had been—Jezebel's son.

"Go ahead, Joram! Why should killing Elisha in front of her be any worse than stealing her family's lands?" Nahum came toward him and threw the bulky sack at his feet. When it hit the floor, the string around its opening came loose and the contents spilled out onto the floor.

Joram took a step backward and stared down at seven pairs of his own sandals.

"You're a liar and a thief, Joram of Israel!" Nahum charged.

The light-and-shadow play from the torch in Joram's hand painted a hellish, grotesque expression on his face. "I should have killed you long ago, farmer, and taken what was rightfully mine!" He pulled his dagger and holding the torch in front of himself like a shield, advanced on Nahum.

Nahum stood his ground.

"No!" Merari screamed, rushing forward.

Nahum moved to intercept and protect her.

The dagger in Joram's hand flashed downward, viciously. With an agonizingly slow half-turn, Nahum crumpled and fell between Joram and Merari. Blood spurted from the mortal wound in his neck and made a crimson pool on the floor.

Dismayed and disbelieving, Elisha stared at his fallen friend.

A painful moan of denial escaped from Obadiah.

Shock paralyzed Merari. Her eyes saw Nahum's lifeless body. Her mind recognized that life had ebbed from him. But she felt nothing. In that horrible, suspended moment, she, too, sustained a wound too deep to feel.

Joram seemed scarcely to breathe, as if to do so would call down immediate judgment from all the gods. He stared in terror, tacitly acknowledging that once again he had been vanquished in shame by the farmer from Shunem.

Merari dropped to her knees beside Nahum and retrieved the dagger from its deadly resting place as gently as she would draw a briar from a child's hand.

Joram threw down his torch and backed away.

"The horrors of hell will haunt you, Joram of Israel," Elisha said. "You're a whelp of the devil and the devil's bride!"

Joram panicked and fled.

− 17 −

For Merari, the aftermath of Nahum's shocking death was a jumble of mixed memories. After Joram had panicked and fled, Obadiah called two of his trusted household servants, who brought blankets and a litter. Elisha came to her, grasped her shoulders gently, and lifted her to her feet so that the servants could prepare Nahum's body for the night's journey back to Shunem. Ready to leave the courtyard, they ignored the tunnel and went openly through the palace to the northern city gate. No one stopped them. In fact, no one saw them. All of the city and most of the palace staff were swarming the tents deserted by the fleeing Syrians, looting their treasures and stealing their food.

Reaching the tangle of acacias where they had left their horses, they decided that Obadiah would ride to the secret place nearby where the people of Shunem waited with the carts of grain. Elisha, meanwhile, would lead Merari and the servants with Nahum's body directly back to Shunem. The journey that had started as such an adventure in search of justice was concluding as a cortege of heartbreak. For Merari, time no longer mattered. The anesthesia which the human heart provides for itself in times of mourning had taken over, allowing her to move about, to converse with Elisha and Obadiah's two servants from the palace—but, mercifully, to feel nothing. Its effects were more long-lasting than she would ever have thought. It helped her through the rigors of greeting friends and neighbors who came to the compound for Nahum's burial. It consoled her through the tearful farewells when she and Elisha, Uncle

Obadiah, Tamar, Gehazi, and Kallai set out for Joppa; gave her the comfort of happy, cherished memories; led her in a careful tiptoe around other memories too freshly painful to confront. And, when she faced the sternest task of all— telling Ozem and Hakkatan how Nahum had died, and finding a way to comfort them in their sorrow and in their anger—the anesthesia of grief stood her in good stead, even then.

As others' tears mingled with hers, solace came to them all. In spite of the alien emptiness of a future no longer filled with shared dreams, hearts and minds finally began to accept the reality of Nahum's death.

For her father and Uncle Obadiah, Nahum's death brought to a close a lifetime of service to the royal court of Israel. A messenger had been sent from Shunem to Benaiah in Phoenicia, telling him of the death and urging him to return at once to the family in Joppa. A second message had been sent to Zibia, announcing the return of Elisha and Merari.

When they finally arrived in Joppa, Elisha, so strong and constant in his support of Merari, now sought the isolation of prayer and meditation to heal his own heart. "I want to take vengeance on Joram," he confided to Merari, "yet I must not. Vengeance belongs to the Lord."

Scarcely had the period of his meditations passed when he announced his intention to go to Ramoth-Gilead. "A great battle is taking place there," he explained to the family. "Joram is now fighting Hazael and his Syrians. Jezebel has returned to Jezreel. The Lord is instructing me to go; he is leading me to Ramoth-Gilead. The time draws nigh for the prophecy of Elijah to be fulfilled. The Lord is telling me to anoint Joram's successor."

"I want to travel with you, Elisha," Ozem said.

"And I, too," Hakkatan quickly added. "Jehu will be in Ramoth-Gilead, won't he?"

"I cannot take you with me, my sons. Your mother needs

you with her. It may be months—even years—before the fighting is finished."

"Should we not have a chance to avenge my father?" Ozem's earnest young face tore at Elisha's heart.

He knelt down to be eye-to-eye with the lad. "That's the Lord's job. He has told us not to avenge ourselves, remember?"

Disappointment crossed the faces of both boys.

Elisha stood up and put his hands on their shoulders. "Someday you will understand better. One day, you will understand the Lord's wisdom for your lives." He turned and looked at Ozem. "You must begin to take more and more of the family responsibility on yourself. Your grandfather grows older. So does your Uncle Obadiah. There's much you must learn from them in order to care for your mother and all the others. It will be your special task, Ozem. Do you understand?"

Ozem nodded. "I understand, but . . . I shall miss you, Elisha."

"We all will," Hakkatan added.

Merari came to him and touched his hand. "Godspeed your journey, my friend. Come back to us soon. Until then, all will be well."

The most direct route to Ramoth-Gilead lay through the land of Israel. But rather than risk going back into the Northern Kingdom, Elisha and Gehazi took a longer way through Judah. They bypassed Jerusalem to the north, cutting down through the Kidron Valley, and following the Jericho Road eastward. They stopped for food and rest at the prophets' school in Jericho and asked two of the young prophets to travel on with them from there. By twilight of the sixth day after leaving Joppa, they approached the southern edge of the Israelite camp and found a camping place in a secluded stand of acacias. Leaving the two young prophets to prepare a meal, they went on to find Commander Jehu.

"Why must we see him, master? He'll be near to the king. And you know the king will kill you if he gets the chance."

"If you're frightened, Gehazi, then go stay at the campsite. The young prophets will protect you!" Elisha kicked his horse into a trot.

A chastened and silent servant followed, until at last they had made their way almost completely through the string of Israelite tents and campfires. Men and animals were straggling back into the camp from the day's fighting. Chariots rumbled by, churning up dirt. "The fighting must've been hard today," Elisha commented, more to himself than to Gehazi. "These men look bone-weary."

"Master, there! Commander Jehu's tent must be there." He pointed left.

Elisha reined in. Two tents larger than all the others, and a third even larger tent, loomed on the horizon. Elisha dismounted and led his horse. Gehazi did likewise. Another chariot came slowly from the direction in which the battle had taken place. It came so slowly, in fact, that it appeared as if both horses and driver were weary of war and weary of violence. The charioteer leaned against the railing of the chariot in a posture of exhaustion.

"That's Commander Jehu, master."

"I can see that it is. Come." He quickened his pace and went to meet the chariot. "Commander! A moment there!"

The charioteer straightened and reined to a halt.

Elisha moved up closer and pushed back the hood of his robe. Jehu frowned and peered at him through the deepening twilight.

"It is your friend, Elisha. The prophet."

Jehu straightened. "You're in danger here, prophet. Have a care."

"Where can we talk?" Elisha asked, lowering his voice.

"In my tent. Come along."

They left a nervous Gehazi outside with the horses and entered the tent. Jehu's servant lighted a small lamp, set it

on a table, and silently left. Elisha and Jehu went to the table
and sat down.

"I'm glad to see you, Elisha." Removing his helmet, Jehu
picked up a wine flask, poured two cups, and handed one
to Elisha. "A friendly face brightens this day. Especially
after today's battle."

Elisha accepted the cup of wine and saluted the commander. "Then the battle is going badly?"

"Aye. And very badly today. We've sent for King Ahaziah of Judah to come and help us." He gulped at his wine
and poured another cup. "Today's battle could be called a
defeat, I suppose. Joram was wounded."

Elisha glanced up in surprise. "Joram? Wounded?"

Jehu nodded.

"How seriously?"

"He bled rather badly. We propped him up in his chariot
so the enemy wouldn't know. And, for that matter, so our
own men wouldn't know. We wanted no panic."

"Just like his father," Elisha murmured, recalling that the
same deceptive action had been taken for Ahab when he
had been mortally wounded here at Ramoth-Gilead years
before.

"Where's Joram now?"

"He's being carried to Jezreel." The tone was flat, unsympathetic.

"Jezreel?"

"Aye. Samaria is too far. As I said, he was bleeding
heavily. A physician in the palace at Jezreel has much experience with such wounds as Joram's."

"And Jezebel is in Jezreel also, is she not?"

Jehu gave a peculiar laugh. "That is my understanding."

Elisha stared in silence for a moment at the flame of the
lamp, realizing how precisely the words of the Lord were
beginning to be manifested in human actions and circum-
stances.

"But enough of war talk," Jehu said. "What brings you
here to this scene of misery?"

"The Lord told me to come."

"Oh?" Jehu leaned back with a grin. "I hope he told you to bring me good news from home."

Elisha fingered the rim of his cup, realizing that Jehu had not yet heard of Nahum's death.

"How's the boy Hakkatan? And all the rest of that wonderful family? Are they still in Joppa? It's been a long time since I've heard any news of them."

Elisha hesitated and searched for a gentle way to tell Jehu about it. But there really was no gentle way. Nahum's death had not been gentle.

Jehu frowned at the hesitation. "Hakkatan is all right, isn't he?"

"Oh, yes. The boy is fine."

"Then what is it? Something troubles you."

"There has been a death in the family."

"Who?"

"Nahum."

Jehu's eyes widened with astonishment.

"He was killed."

"Killed? By whom?"

"By Joram."

Jehu's jaw went slack; his eyes revealed disbelief.

Without further hesitation, Elisha filled in the details. As he finished relating the full account of the tragedy, Jehu made a fist of one hand and hammered it down on the table. The flame in the lamp wavered and flickered. "Son of a she-devil! What misery!" He got up and paced back and forth like a caged beast.

The intensity of his reaction was surprising—almost as surprising, Elisha thought, as his apparent lack of concern over Joram's battle wounds.

Jehu swore and turned toward him. "What's being done about it?"

"What can be done? Joram is king."

"But is he God?"

"No, he isn't God. But we must bide our time, Jehu.

Joram's fate is in the hands of the Lord. The Lord's instructions were made clear to me. We must bide our time."

Jehu started to argue, but Elisha held up his hand. "We must trust and obey the Lord."

"To trust the Lord in times like these is hard to do." Jehu said.

"But trust him we must," Elisha repeated. "There's no other way. For you, or for me, or for Israel."

With a heavy sigh, the commander turned away. "It shall be as you say, Prophet. It shall be as you say. Contact me when you need me."

Elisha spent the next two full days in deepest prayer and meditation during which time the whispering voice spoke almost constantly to his spirit. Its revelations of the present, the future, and the far reaches of time were vivid and explicit. He was to anoint Joram's successor. And this night, was the time. All else would evolve from that.

Elisha arose from his secluded spot and went toward the campfire. Gehazi and the two young prophets were huddled near the fire to ward off the evening's sudden chill. Elisha stood looking at them, momentarily uncertain which of them he should take with him into the town of Ramoth-Gilead.

Once again, the whispering voice spoke to his spirit. He turned and motioned for the youngest of the prophets to come with him. The lad rose and followed him until they reached a house at the edge of the town. There, a number of the Israelite officers were having supper.

Elisha halted and reached into his robe to pull forth a small flask filled with oil. He turned to the young prophet. "Take this flask of oil in your hand with care. I want you to go into this house and ask for Commander Jehu. Make him rise up from his fellow officers and go with you into another room. When you're alone with him, take the flask of oil, pour it on his head, and say to him these words: 'Thus says the Lord God of Israel: I have anointed you king over the people of the Lord, over Israel. You shall strike down the house of Ahab that I may avenge the blood of my servants, the prophets, and the blood of all the servants of the Lord at the hand of Jezebel.

" 'The whole house shall perish. And dogs shall eat Jezebel in the vicinity of Jezreel, and there shall be none to bury her.'

"Those are the words you are to say to Commander Jehu, young prophet. And when you have said those words, you are to open the door and flee. Do not delay."

The eyes of the young prophet were wide and alight with awe at his task.

"Do you understand it all?"

"Yes, sir."

"I shall wait for you here, near this window. Go now."

The young prophet did as he had been instructed and quickly returned to where Elisha waited. Through the window, they saw Jehu return to his fellow officers.

"Is all well?" asked one of the officers, noticing how Jehu brushed at the oil which had dripped onto his robes. "What did that madman do to you? Why did he come to you?"

Jehu tried to evade their questions, so new to him was the idea of being king.

But they were persistent. Finally, he told them all that the young prophet had done and said.

There was a momentary hush.

"He has anointed you King of Israel?" Captain Bidkar, an old friend, asked.

Jehu nodded.

The house at the edge of Ramoth-Gilead rocked with the shouts of approval from all the officers in it. Each man hastened to take off his outer cloak and put it down on the floor so that Jehu might walk on it, signifying his dominion and authority. At the same time, the act signified each man's loyalty to Jehu. They blew trumpets. And they shouted as if in one great voice, "Jehu is king! Jehu is king!"

Hours later, Jehu came to where Elisha was camped in

the secluded stand of acacias. "You know what has happened?"

"I know." Elisha pointed to the young prophet. "I sent him to you."

Jehu smiled and grasped his arm. "I ride this night to Jezreel, to begin to carry out the instructions of the Lord. Will you ride with me, Prophet, and witness that the evil in the land is being destroyed?"

"I will ride with you. But first I must bid farewell to the young prophets and to Gehazi."

"I'll wait," Jehu agreed.

Elisha went to Gehazi. "Carry this message to Merari and to her son. Say to them Nahum's death is avenged!"

Gehazi's eyes bulged.

"Do you understand?"

"Yes, master."

"Then you are to return to Shunem to be with your wife until I return."

"Yes, master."

Elisha then went with Jehu.

The sun was well up by the time the walls of the palace at Jezreel came into view. Jehu's chariots pulled to a halt on a small rise to let the horses rest for a bit. They could see the palace very clearly—even the watchmen on the tower.

Jehu turned to Elisha. "When we move forward once more, you must get down on the floorboards, lest they see you and attempt to kill you."

Elisha nodded, then pointed to the palace. "They have seen us. One of the watchmen hurries from his tower."

"To report to Joram, no doubt." Jehu stepped down from the chariot and began walking about, stretching and refreshing himself from the journey. Others in the company did likewise.

The watchman reappeared on the tower, and a horseman came toward them from the city gate.

Elisha climbed back onto Jehu's chariot and hunkered down so that the man couldn't see him.

Jehu walked out to meet the horseman, sword drawn. "Hail, Commander! Thus the king says, 'Is it peace?' "

Jehu laughed. "What have you to do with peace? Turn around and follow me."

The horseman did so without further persuasion.

The watchman disappeared from the tower a second time; and soon a second horseman came through the city gate and rode toward them.

Again, sword drawn, Jehu went to meet the horseman. "Hail, Commander! Thus says the king, 'Is it peace?' "

And again Jehu answered, "What have you to do with peace? Turn around and follow me."

The horseman did so and joined the first horseman at the rear of the group of chariots.

"Now what, Jehu?" asked one of his captains.

"Let us drive forward. At a furious pace. Let us drive to that land there." He pointed to a beautiful garden area which had a large open space on its nearest side. "That land once belonged to Naboth. He was a friend. He was a good man. Jezebel cheated him out of his property and had him killed. Let us drive onto that land and wait for Joram to come to us."

"You think he will come, Commander?"

"I think he will come." He climbed back up into his chariot and led the group to the land that once had belonged to Naboth. And there, they waited.

The wait was not a long one.

Joram, King of Israel, and Ahaziah, King of Judah, came out. Each in his own chariot, they came out to meet Jehu and his company on the property of Naboth, the Jezreelite.

Joram leaned heavily against the railing of his chariot and looked much as he had when they propped him up after he had been wounded. But his voice was strong. "Hail, Jehu! Is it peace?"

"What peace?" Jehu answered. "What peace, indeed, as long as your mother's harlotries and acts of witchcraft are so many?"

Joram's face went white.

"Where is Jezebel, Joram?" Jehu demanded. "Where is your mother? She's back in Israel, isn't she? She's there in the palace in Jezreel, isn't she?"

Joram swore.

Ahaziah looked at him in astonishment, fear climbing into his face.

Joram struggled to straighten up. He tried to quickly turn his horses. But they responded sluggishly. "Ahaziah, flee. It is treachery! Treachery!"

Ahaziah whipped his horses into action and fled in a southerly direction.

"Follow him," Jehu ordered. "Destroy him! He is of Joram's family."

Two of the company of chariots went chasing after the King of Judah.

Joram still struggled to turn his horses.

Jehu pulled his bow from his shoulder, fitted it with an arrow, and aimed at Joram. With his full strength, he let fly the arrow.

It found its mark swiftly and surely in the middle of the left side of Joram's back and came out at his heart. Without a sound he sank down in his chariot.

"Pick him up and throw him out onto the field of Naboth," Jehu commanded. Two of the captains did so at once.

Elisha stood up now in the chariot of Jehu and began to recite the words of the Lord. "Surely I saw yesterday the blood of Naboth and the blood of his sons; and I will repay you in this plot!"

Signalling the rest of his company, Jehu moved forward toward the city of Jezreel; through the city gates and down the narrow, deserted streets they drove to the courtyard of the palace itself.

A woman's voice called down from an upper window. "Is it peace, Jehu of Zimri, murderer of your master?"

He looked up.

Jezebel stood at the window. She had put paint on her eyes and had adorned her head with the implements of royalty. "Well, Jehu of Zimri, answer me. Is it peace?"

Jehu ignored her and shouted instead, "Who is on my side? Who in the palace is on the side of Jehu?"

From another window, very close to the one Jezebel looked down from, appeared the faces of two eunuchs. "Here, Commander. We're with you!"

Jezebel grimaced, scorning them.

"Throw her down!" Jehu ordered.

They moved toward her.

Elisha pushed back the hood of his robes, fully revealing his face. His bald head glistened in the morning sunlight.

When Jezebel saw Elisha, her scornful grimace changed to a look of fear. The eunuchs grabbed her. She resisted, struggled against them—but without success. In another instant, her body hit the cobblestones of the courtyard with a sickening thud. Blood spattered from her, frightening the horses. They reared and pranced about, neighing and whinnying and trampling the body of Jezebel under their feet.

Two of Jehu's captains pulled them off the body and quieted them. Others went forward to cover Jezebel's remains.

"Leave her," Jehu ordered, climbing down from his chariot and removing his helmet. "You're tired. Thirsty and hungry. Come and rest yourselves before you bury the dead. You too, Prophet." He turned and led the way into the palace.

Elisha followed, impressed with the authority of the man.

Jehu greeted the palace staff cordially but firmly, announcing his intention to discuss their employment later. "For the moment, you will serve me and my men as you would serve any other king! For I am now your king. Anointed by the Lord God Jehovah. Bring food and drink for my men."

The servants did as they were told, bringing copious amounts of food and drink. From the looks of the table before them, one would never have guessed that a famine strangled the land.

Elisha excused himself and went to a far quiet corner of the great dining hall to offer up a prayer of thanksgiving and praise. "Oh Lord God of creation's good things, we praise your holy name. We thank you for giving us the choice to do your will, and for surrounding us with men and women of faith, of good intent, and of loyalty to your words. We ask your continuing blessings for all those who seek to do your will—especially for Merari, Ozem, Hakkatan, Benaiah, Obadiah, and Zibia; for Gehazi and Tamar and their unborn child. And, O Lord, we ask you to bless the leadership of Jehu. Help him to lead Israel out of the famine and the drouth, and out of the ways of evil worship. Amen."

"Amen," came Jehu's rumbling voice right beside him.

Elisha turned in surprise. The big man had moved so quietly that he hadn't heard him. But there he stood, a serious look in his eyes.

Behind him stood all his men, with their heads still bowed as they finished their own prayers.

"Thank you, Prophet. Come now, let us share the food."

As they started back to the tables, the two captains who had quieted the horses approached. "Shouldn't we bury Jezebel's remains, Commander?"

"Before you've rested and had your food?"

"We'd like to get it over with, sir."

Elisha interrupted. "You'll find nothing to bury."

"Why not?" asked Jehu.

"Because of the prophecy of the prophet Elijah."

"And what was that?"

"The Lord told Elijah that there would be nothing left when Jezebel was killed. The dogs would eat her flesh; the corpse of Jezebel would be refuse at Jezreel so that she could not be buried, and so that the people would not be able to say, 'Here lies Jezebel'."

Jehu surveyed Elisha with a long, searching look, then motioned for his captains not to bother about Jezebel.

Elisha, however, sure of his knowledge from Elijah, and also certain in his heart that the captains did not believe him, said, "Go, look for yourselves."

Jehu agreed, and the captains left the dining hall. Soon they returned with the report that all they found of Jezebel was her skull, her hands, and her feet.

In a manner of great respect, Jehu stood up and saluted Elisha. All the company joined in.

Elisha nodded, accepting the salute. "Be obedient to the Lord," he said, "and the land of Israel will prosper."

They all reseated themselves and began their meal in a weary silence. The fatigue of battle, and the shock of the events of the morning combined with the food and wine to create a reflective mood among them. By twos and threes, they quietly talked together. Some said nothing at all, simply resting for the first time in days.

Jehu leaned close to Elisha. A lonely, haunted look was in his eyes. "I should like to have Hakkatan live with me now. As king, I will not have to fight as many battles as I did as a charioteer. But would I have the right to ask Merari to return him to me so soon after Nahum's death?"

Elisha was touched at the big man's concern for Merari's feelings. "I will go to her in the proper season and inquire," he offered.

Jehu nodded. "Now that Jezebel is dead, all children will be safer in Israel."

"And now that Joram is dead," Elisha added, "Merari can return to her own land and her home in Shunem."

"Will she want to return?"

Elisha reflected for only a moment. "She is a strong woman, Jehu. A woman of great heart. A woman of great faith. She will want to come back, I think."

And so it was in due time, and in the proper season, that Elisha went to Joppa to fetch Merari and all her family to bring them to the royal court of Jehu, King of Israel, at the Ivory Palace in Samaria.

More than a full year had passed since Nahum's death.

As Merari stepped from the magnificent throne room into the long gallery adjacent to the king's private court-yard, she hesitated. She dreaded being here. Why had Jehu insisted on holding his audience with them here in the courtyard? Didn't he know what stark memories it held for her? And why had Elisha not persuaded him to hold it elsewhere? She glanced at her old friend walking beside her and realized that it must be hard for him, too, to be in this place where Nahum had been so cruelly struck down. At her other side walked Hakkatan and Ozem. Behind her, she heard a muffled sob from her mother, and heard her father and Uncle Obadiah comfort her.

They were well into the courtyard now, passing the foun-tain beside which Nahum had fallen. She turned to look at the spot where his blood had seeped onto the ivory inlay, as if half expecting to see it still there. It was not, of course. The floor was scrubbed clean and beautiful. She glanced at the boys. They, too, were looking in the direction of the fountain, sad resolve in their eyes. They had grown so tall. Soon they would be men, Merari realized. The future was theirs. Nahum was past. Not to be forgotten, but neither to be mourned forever. Maybe it was best, after all, that this first meeting with Jehu as king be held here. Maybe the peace and beauty of the place which she had known as a child could become a part of the boys' good memories, too. Perhaps Jehu was far wiser than she had realized.

He approached now from his private chambers. Enor-mous pride showed in his face as he looked at both of the boys and smiled at them.

They bowed.

He turned, acknowledged the presence of her mother and father and Uncle Obadiah, saluted Elisha, and then came to her. "Thank you for coming, Merari, and for bring-ing your family."

She bowed.

"I wanted to see you again to say thank you. With all my heart, I thank you for your capacity to love and care for

Hakkatan as your own. And now . . . to give him back to me."

She trembled.

Elisha took her hand and held it tightly.

"You already know," Jehu went on, "that the lands of Shunem still belong to you and your family. But I want you to know, also, that they are safe now. You can move back to them."

Tears brimmed in her eyes.

"And safe they shall remain for you, and for all your family, for as long as I am king."

An almost inaudible sob escaped her.

Ozem edged closer and slipped his arm around her. "All is well, my mother. Once again, all is well!"

I f you enjoyed this book, you will want to read our other captivating biblical novels. Look for them at your bookstore or call us at 800-638-3030. We accept Master-Card, VISA, and personal checks.

Novels by bestselling author Lois T. Henderson

HAGAR

"Poignant... moving... makes the Bible a vital document about people whose emotions and faith we feel."—*Gladys Taber*

MIRIAM

"Lois T. Henderson has become America's leading writer of biblical fiction.... She takes pains to be historically accurate, yet she writes in an imaginative and engaging way. *Miriam* makes for absorbing reading while providing spiritual insight."—*Christian Herald*

RUTH

"Lois Henderson again displays her special talent for weaving drama and history together. She has taken the brief biblical account of [Ruth] and written a fast-moving, compelling story. Henderson has stayed mainly with the biblical story but has rounded [it] out with additional characters in keeping with the times.... She faithfully portrays Ruth's courage as she leaves her homeland and begins her encounters with a new religion and culture."—*The Christian Librarian*

ABIGAIL

"Beautiful! Inspiring! The author's special talent clothes the Bible with meaning and makes it live."—*Dr. Kenneth L. Wilson*

LYDIA

"Readers step into the New Testament to experience the conflicts and joys of Lydia's newfound faith."—*Virtue*

PRISCILLA AND AQUILA

Lois Henderson's final novel, completed by coauthor Harold Ivan Smith after her death, tells the triumphant story of the New Testament heroine Priscilla, whose wisdom, courage, and faith make her a model for today.